Also by Peter Cave and
available from Redemption Books

Chopper

Mama
by Peter Cave

REDEMPTION
BOOKS

First published in the UK
by New English Library, 1972.
This edition published by Redemption Books, 1995.
A division of Redemption Films Limited,
BCM PO Box 9235, London WC1N 3XX.

Copyright © Peter Cave 1972.
The right of Peter Cave to be identified as author of this work has been asserted by him in accordance with the Copyright, Designs and Patents Act 1988.

Introduction copyright
© Maz Harris, Hells Angels MC, England.

Photographic illustrations copyright
© Redemption Books 1995.

A catalogue record for this book is available from the British Library.

ISBN 1 899634 15 0

All rights reserved. No part of this publication may be reproduced, stored in a retrieval system, or transmitted, in any form or by any means, electronic, mechanical, photocopying, recording or otherwise, without the prior permission of the Publishers.

This book is sold subject to the condition that it shall not, by way of trade or otherwise, be lent, re-sold, hired out, or otherwise circulated without the Publisher's prior consent in any form of binding or cover other than that in which it is published and without a similar condition including this condition being imposed on the subsequent purchaser.

Printed in the UK by
The Guernsey Press Company Limited.
Cover and photographic section printed by
Colin Clapp Printers.

INTRODUCTION

When I was asked to write an introduction to **Redemption's** reprint of *Peter Cave's* cult classics, **Chopper** and **Mama,** I was, I confess, cautious. Why anyone would want to publish, let alone purchase, these tales of bad boy bikers, a quarter of a century on, was a mystery to me.

I didn't dismiss it out of hand, however, I was intrigued and, being of an inquisitive turn of mind, I decided to delve deeper. Rummaging through the attic, I found what I was looking for... a complete collection of biker fiction bearing the *New English Library* logo. Why I've hung on to them, I've no idea. Maybe I'm sentimental. Maybe I thought that, one day, they'd make me some money. But hang on to them I have. As, I suspect, have many of my generation who, though they've moved on a mite since the seventies, can't quite bring themselves to dispence with the trappings of their teens. I flicked through the well-thumbed pages, to familiarise myself with the plot, and found myself stepping back in time, to the days when I knew nothing about bikers, but desired, desperately, to learn.

Chopper appeared in the shops in 1971; **Mama**, twelve months later. Both were best-sellers. Why? The answer is obvious. Look at the covers. Look at the impact they must have had on young, impressionable minds — mine included. Sure the characters are far-fetched. Sure their exploits are exaggerated beyond belief. But, back then, that was what we wanted. And, sad to say, we couldn't get enough of it. We didn't want to be told that the rest of our lives would be taken up with trying to make ends meet; that marriage, mortgage and middle age would follow in swift succession. We wanted to make an impact. We wanted to walk on the wild side. We wanted to take the world by the balls and twist it till it begged for mercy. And if we couldn't break through the barrier, between us and our aspirations, well we'd read about others who had, even if it was mostly a myth.

The novels of *Peter Cave* are as far removed from the reality of the British bike scene as westerns are from the reality of riding the range. The history of the **Hell Angels** owes nothing to flights of fancy. We need no books to tell us how to live our lives. We never have, and we never will. And if anyone imagines, for one fleeting moment, that enlightenment can be found in the pages of paperback pulp, then they've an awful lot to learn. *Chopper* and *Mama* are part of our past only insofar as they were instrumental in shaping the public's perception of us, the *Hells Angels.* Read them, by all means. Enjoy them, for what they are. But remember, the truth is stranger still.

Maz Harris.
Hell Angels MC England.
October 1995

CHAPTER ONE — FUNERAL

'**Chopper' Harris was dead. The black coffin containing his mangled body slid along the conveyor belt into the crematorium, where the oxygen-fed flames would reduce it and its contents to a small pile of grey, unidentifiable ashes.**

The small, select group of mourners looked upon the scene almost dispassionately. His parents, stooped over with age and a crushing sense of resignation, were years beyond grief at their son's abrupt departure from the world. At the age of sixteen they had lost him, somewhere in that huge void of non-communication between different generations. His death, eight years later, seemed like only the final confirmation of a fact they already knew.

Several assorted relatives, a couple of friends who had worked with him in the factory and a disinterested vicar watched the coffin disappear from view and then turned their backs. It was over, but for the ceremonious presentation of the small urn containing the ashes.

If a Hells Angel had a soul, then Chopper's would at that moment be screaming with anger and frustration.

This was not the way he would have chosen to go...laid out in his box dressed in a faded, conservative blue serge suit. Chopper would have wanted to lie in state, resplendent in his Angel originals and colours which he had worn so proudly in life. He would have chosen a funeral in true Hells Angel tradition - with the coffin borne into the cemetery grounds across two powerful motorbikes, with a faint wintery sun reflecting from the polished steel helmets of his compatriots.

And of even this, Chopper Harris was cheated - cheated just as he had been during the last few moments of his brief life. He had fought a battle, won it and lost everything in the space of a few hours. Death had cheated him of his moment of triumph, and now his funeral cheated him of the last chance of glory.

Only the flames of the crematorium might have warmed his soul...for as a Hells Angel, he had been in name and character a natural inhabitant of that nether world of fire and brimstone.

Outside the heavy iron gates of the crematorium, a solemn line of friends and fellow-riders sat upon their powerful hogs and cursed Chopper's parents for refusing them entrance. Even Danny the Deathlover, who would normally have been grinning at the reflected glory of a funeral, was unusually morose.

He turned to his fellow Angels and muttered sadly.

'At least he died with two wheels under him and his colours on his back.'

It was a small crumb of comfort to them all.

At the head of the line of Angels, Marty Gresham sat rigidly upright in his saddle. His face was impassive, set in a grim mask of defiance because he knew that the others resented his presence. Chopper had been his best friend - but that friendship had come to a sudden end on the night of Chopper's death. Both he and Chopper had fought for the leadership of the Hells Angels, and he had lost.

On the night, any feelings of kinship they had once shared had turned to hate and disgust...and that hate had led Chopper to his untimely death, lying smashed and bleeding under the wreckage of Marty's hog.

For several minutes Marty sat motionless. Finally he swung his leg over the saddle, propped the hog up on its footrest and dismounted. Summoning all the dignity he could muster, Marty peeled off his set of Hells Angels originals and laid them carefully over the black saddle of the borrowed hog. Finally, he unfastened the Nazi helmet from his head and placed it on top.

Big M, alias Marty Gresham, was no more. For him, the Hells Angels suddenly ceased to exist. For Chopper, who had been his friend, this last farewell had been a gesture of reverence. There would be no more hell-raising, no more speed and thrills with a powerful machine between his legs.

Marty walked slowly away from the assembled group without a backwards glance. No one said a word, or bade him goodbye. Perhaps, underneath their resentment, they had understood. He walked slowly down the road from the crematorium, leaving the Hells Angels behind him and stepping forward into the world of the ordinary citizen which he had rejected for so long.

Long after he had disappeared from view, Danny the Deathlover finally kicked his hog into roaring life and wheeled it around.

'Let's go and have a bloody drink,' he muttered moodily, and let his clutch out fiercely. The Angels followed him, their wheels tearing up the gravel of the crematorium driveway.

CHAPTER TWO

PHOENIX

Elaine Willsman sat in the loneliness of her tiny bed-sitter and wondered if it was all over. She had wanted to go to the funeral, but her overwhelming sense of guilt had rendered her incapable when the time came. Like Lady Macbeth, she felt as though she had a murderer's hands - stained with blood which would never wash away. Chopper Harris was dead, Marty Gresham was banished...and she was responsible for it all. She had been a leader's girl, eager to follow and distribute her sexual favours to the victor in the battle.

...Only in this battle, there had been no victor. Only two vanquished enemies who had once been friends. Marty was defeated by her denunciation of him and Chopper was beaten by death - the ultimate conqueror.

For the hundredth time, she took a small photograph of Chopper from her handbag and gazed at it. The tears welled up once again in her eyes, blurring the image of the smiling, defiant face and the aggressive, powerful lines of the bike upon which he sat so proudly.

Suddenly all the guilt and bitterness rose in her throat and threatened to choke her. Deep inside, Elaine suddenly discovered a smouldering heap of frustrations which were about to erupt into a blazing fire.

'I'll make it up to you, Chopper,' she vowed silently to the image in the photograph. 'I swear I'll avenge you.'

Even as she made her bitter vows, Elaine felt the sudden weight of a crushing responsibility descend upon her. A sense of vocation, a calling, a little voice inside her head telling her exactly what she had to do was born...and Elaine knew that now, it would never die.

Struck with this new knowledge, Elaine's tears ceased abruptly. She rose, crossing the tiny room to the wardrobe in which her meagre collection of clothes were untidily piled. Hastily, she pulled them out and scattered them around the floor. She ripped dressed from hangers, not caring if buttons popped off or the cloth tore.

Dresses, skirts, frilly blouses...anything remotely feminine was discarded, flung across the room into a pile bound for the dustbin. A couple of brassieres came to light. Elaine flung one on to

3

the pile, then hesitated with the second pair in her hand.

She looked at the tiny garment for a few seconds, then laughed, flinging it to join its condemned twin.

She reached up behind her back, under the thick wool sweater and fumbled with the clasp of the bra she was wearing. Deftly unclipping it, she pulled it away from her full, firm young breasts and added it to the unwanted junk.

She crossed to the small mirror over her dressing table and appraised herself carefully. Throwing out her chest, Elaine moved sensuously and looked at her own reflection with a sense of pride. She didn't need the brassieres - her perfect figure could stand up well, without the need for such artificial support.

Returning to the wardrobe, Elaine fished through the remaining bits and pieces of clothing until she came to what she wanted. A black, one-piece leather suit which zipped from the crotch right up to the neck. Eagerly casting off her sweater and jeans, Elaine stepped gingerly into the leggings of the suit and virtually poured herself into the tight-fitting outfit. It clung to her like a second skin, clinging to every curve and accentuating her sensual figure.

She pulled up the gleaming chromium zipper to her throat, revelling in the sexy feel of the cool leather against her bare flesh. A pair of matching leather boots and black gloves completed the outfit.

Wriggling lasciviously inside the form-hugging costume, Elaine slithered, snake-like across the room once more. Taking a nylon hairbrush from the dressing table, she brushed her long golden hair until it hung in glossy, luxurious waves over the neck of the black suit and down over her shoulders. This completed, she dared to look at her reflection in the mirror.

Elaine couldn't help a smile of self-satisfaction. The total effect of the outfit was absolutely stunning - her golden tresses clashing dramatically with the dull sheen of the black leather.

It looked sexy, yet aggressive...almost a contradictory visual statement. The overall effect of the leather was masculine, virile, but it drew attention to the proud swell of her breasts, the tightness of her narrow waist and the smooth, rounded shape of her hips and buttocks.

Already plans were buzzing through Elaine's head. She could

see herself flying down the motorway, her mane of hair blowing in the wind behind her. She could imagine the throbbing power of a powerful hog engine between her thighs. Better still, she could imagine twenty, thirty...a hundred Angels riding behind her, dealing out mayhem, violence and retribution whenever and wherever they saw fit.

Elaine smiled inwardly, rubbing the palms of her hands against the front of the black leather suit. She would make the Angels everything that Chopper had wanted them to be - and perhaps more. She would knock them out of their sense of lazy complacency which Big M had allowed to fester in their midst. With Elaine as the leader, the Hells Angels would be a force to be reckoned with, an army without fear or favour, a crusading band of renegades dedicated to the violence of revolution and social disruption.

Suddenly, Elaine snapped out of her daydream and laughed. It seemed funny that the black leather suit she wore created such ideas. It had been a birthday present from Marty.

There was only one vital thing missing...a hog. In the dream it was painted jet black - black like her costume, and the gleaming chromium of the ape-handlebars and the exhaust pipes glittered with fire. In reality she had nothing, and no immediate chance of procuring one.

Elaine fished in the drawers and eventually drew out her Post Office Savings Book. Dejectedly, she totted up her entire life savings. Fifty-three pounds and a few pennies! She sat down miserably on the edge of her bed and bitter frustration started to well up inside her once again.

...But: There was one faint chance! Her face brightened. Fired by impulse, Elaine scooped up the savings book, threw some things into a black shoulder bag and let herself out of the flatlet. Stopping only at the Post Office to draw out the money, she headed straight for Bernie's dubious little garage in a Walthamstow back-street.

Bernie was a friend of the Angels. Too old to ride any more, his love of motorbikes had never faded, and he happily spent his time repairing damaged hogs, or re-spraying and disguising stolen ones. He was the unofficial repairman of the London Angels, the guy who could take a beaten-up old engine and retune it until it could fly.

...And somewhere, in Bernie's garage, was something very precious.

The minute she walked into the scruffy little garage, Elaine saw the hog - and a tiny thrill of power surged through her body. It lay in one corner, just a twisted, mangled heap of metal covered in black oil and dirt from the greasy garage floor.

Marty's Harley-Davidson. The bike on which Chopper had ridden to his death. Untouched since the crash, it had been removed by Bernie as a matter of course. All Angel bikes came to Bernie's...it was an unwritten law.

The garage seemed deserted. Elaine walked in, stood over the remains of the Harley and called through the tiny window at the back.

'Be right wiv ya,' called back a raucous cockney voice. Elaine waited a few moments until the back door opened and Bernie walked in.

He wiped one black, oil-covered hand over his face, only serving to further the filth which obscured his chubby, happy features.

'Ere, it's Elaine, ain't it?' he said with pleasure in his voice. 'I didn't hardly recognise ya in that fancy gear.'

Bernie gazed approvingly at the black suit.

'How are ya gal?'

Elaine smiled. 'I'm fine, Bernie. How's you?'

Under his black mask, Bernie beamed visibly. Elaine had always known how much Bernie had fancied her...she had only to look into his eyes to see the lusting looks he had always thrown at her when Marty wasn't looking. Now, she could put that lust to good advantage.

'How's things wiv the Angels...' Bernie started to say, and then remembered. His face fell, the beaming smile vanished as he glanced down at the pile of scrap metal by Elaine's feet.

'...I'm sorry,' he blurted out awkwardly. 'You know...about Chopper.'

'That's OK Bernie,' Elaine retorted simply.

'He was a good bloke,' Bernie muttered under his breath. 'It was that bloody thing what killed him.'

He gestured violently towards the Harley.

'Poor bastard,' he added vehemently. 'Poor bastard couldn't have had a chance...not wiv them forks buggered up like that.'

Elaine smiled gently, trying to wean him off his morbid thoughts.

'Actually, Bernie...it was about the hog I came to see you. Can it be fixed?'

Bernie looked at her in surprise, then glanced down at the wreck once again.

'Nah. It's a write off,' he said with a shrug. 'I mean - I could do something with it...but who wants to know?'

'I'd be interested,' said Elaine quietly.

Bernie's eyes shrivelled up in puzzlement.

'You? What would you want the bleedin' thing for?'

Elaine shrugged.

'Let's just say...personal reasons,' she replied, 'Anyway...how much?'

Bernie looked at the Harley thoughtfully.

'Needs a hell of a lot of work,' he muttered. 'New front end, a new wheel, handlebars, petrol tank...the top of the cylinder's smashed, rechroming and respray...have to be at least two hundred quid's worth.'

'What about to a friend?' asked Elaine meaningly, bathing Bernie in the warmth of a smile.

Bernie shifted uneasily.

'Well...me time would come cheap of course,' he admitted. 'Sort of sentimental like...if you know what I mean. But the parts alone is going to cost a ton.' He broke off and peered at Elaine closely.

'Are you saying you really want this thing?'

'Yes. That's exactly what I'm saying,' Elaine rejoindered. 'Only I don't have anywhere like that sort of bread.'

Bernie shook his head slowly from side to side. Friends were one thing, but business was business.

'How much ya got then?' he asked at length.

Elaine waved a thin bundle of notes under his nose.

'Fifty now, and I'll owe you the rest for a few weeks,' she promised.

Bernie sucked at his teeth reflectively.

'I don't know...' he muttered. 'I dunno.'

'There's a little bonus on account if you don't trust me,' Elaine said suddenly in a husky voice.

Bernie's eyes shot up to meet hers, flickering nervously.

'What do you mean?'

Elaine's fingers reached upward to her throat and toyed with the fastener on the zip.

'You know what I mean, Bernie.'

She tugged at the zipper gently. It slid slowly downwards, the black leather suit peeling away from her body like the peel from an orange. The zipper was down to her waist now, exposing her unencumbered breasts and the flat smooth plain of her midriff.

Bernie swallowed deeply, running his tongue over his suddenly dry lips. His eyes were glued to the whiteness of Elaine's skin showing through the open suit.

A tiny twitch broke out at one corner of his mouth and flickered neurotically.

'You'd better come into the house,' he muttered at last. 'We'll have to talk about it.'

Elaine smiled wryly, and followed Bernie through the garage.

CHAPTER THREE

BIG MAMA

It was nine o'clock on a Saturday night and the Angels should have been out on the streets of London raising Hell.

Instead, they crowded inside Nick the Greek's tiny, dingy cafe, feeding endless coins into the jukebox and taking turns to beat the one-armed bandit in the corner.

Nick looked up with vague surprise as yet another half-dozen motorcycles roared to a halt outside. He shrugged philosophically, and busied himself splashing boiling water into the tea urn once more. At least he was doing unprecedented business in tea and cokes while the unusual boom lasted.

It had been like this for nearly five weeks now. Every night, the small cafe was packed out with Hells Angels, sitting around moodily and leaving only when the overwhelming sense of boredom became too much for them.

The air was thick with stale tobacco smoke and an almost tangible cloud of depression. Instead of their usual raucous laughter, most of the Angels sat in small groups and conversed in subdued tones.

It was all very strange, and Nick couldn't help wondering when the time-bomb would go off.

Irish Mick fed his last token into the one-armed bandit and pulled the handle. The rows of symbols span round, clicking into place with a losing sequence of mixed fruit.

Irish Mick kicked the side of the machine viciously with the toe of his boot.

"Even this mother-fuggin' fruit machine ain't got no life in it,' he cursed, and made his way back to the dirty, tea-stained table to pore over a cup of cold tea.

Freaky looked up at him blankly, idly scraping accumulated grease and dirt from beneath his fingernails with the business end of a throwing knife.

'I reckon we ought to get some bloody action,' he muttered miserably.

Irish Mick's lips curled into a sneer.

'Like what?' he asked pointedly. 'You gonna be the bright guy who comes up with some ideas?'

Freaky shrugged, and dug at a particularly troublesome piece of grit with the point of the knife.

'Well somebody's got to,' he pointed out unhelpfully.

They both looked optimistically at Danny the Deathlover, who sat opposite. Since Chopper's death, many of the Angels had hopefully assumed that Danny would take control, but for some reason, he seemed loathe to shoulder any responsibility whatsoever.

He grinned at them stupidly for a few seconds.

'I suppose we could go out and see some blood,' he said eventually.

'Shit!' shouted Freaky suddenly, as the point of the knife slipped and carved a small chunk of flesh out of his index finger. He held the afflicted finger up in the air, under Danny's nose.

'Here...here's the only blood you're likely to see tonight,' he murmured ruefully.

Irish Mick's sorrowful face creased into a weak grin.

'You really shouldn't play with blades, Freak,' he chided. 'They're dangerous.'

Reaching over, he snatched the knife from Freaky's fingers and balanced it carefully between thumb and forefinger. He pulled back his wrist into a throwing position and called across the cafe.

'Hey, Nick.'

Nick glanced up from wiping cups a split second before Irish Mick hurled the knife.

As he ducked down behind the safety of his counter with a shrill cry of alarm, the blade buried itself in the wall only a few inches from where his head had been. Ten seconds later, the bald dome of his head re-appeared slowly, his frightened eyes peering round the cafe for further dangers.

Irish Mick dissolved into neurotic laughter. Danny the Deathlover stared moodily at the still-quivering knife for a few seconds and turned towards him with a straight face.

'You missed,' he said flatly, in a playfully mocking voice.

Irish Mick giggled even more insanely and collapsed against the back of his chair.

As the chair rocked up on two legs, Freaky saw his chance for revenge...and took it. Hooking his foot round one of the legs, he pulled viciously so that Irish Mick was hurled backwards to the floor. His laughter ceased abruptly.

'Stupid bastard,' he screamed angrily. 'I might have broken

me bleeding neck.' Irish Mick reached out, grabbed Freaky by the ankles and heaved sideways. Freaky lost his balance, grabbed at a chair and missed and crashed across the table, which promptly collapsed. Freaky, the table and several half-filled cups of tea crashed to the floor while Danny the Deathlover looked on and roared with laughter.

Irish Mick stood up a few seconds before Freaky scrambled to his feet. He was laughing good-naturedly...a laugh which ended suddenly with a yell of pain as Freaky's head butted him hard in the abdomen. He swung down his clenched fist, catching Freaky a glancing blow on the back of the neck.

There was no laughter in the air as Freaky rolled swiftly to one side, jack-knifed up on his knees and sprung to his feet. The two Angels circled each other menacingly, eyes blazing with hate.

Irish Mick reached furtively behind him until his hand encountered the nearest table. With a shove, he sent it sliding back across the floor to make room to move about in.

Suddenly, the atmosphere in the cafe was changed. Everyone present was on their feet, gazing expectantly at the two contestants. The prank had turned into a bitter fight...the boredom had become a sudden thirsting for violence.

It was as if Freaky and Irish Mick had been chosen by the fates to let loose the pent-up frustrations and repressions which had been building up over the last weeks. Suddenly, like a safety valve on a boiler bursting, the tension exploded into violent action.

Freaky reached out one arm and snatched up a half-empty coke bottle from a nearby table. Swinging it high in the air, he smashed it down across the top of a chair. The bottle shattered, leaving Freaky holding a jagged, murderous weapon by its neck. He thrust the broken bottle out at arm's length like a dagger.

Irish Mick's eyes narrowed, and a frown creased his forehead. He'd been preparing for a fight, but not on this level. Backing off, he fumbled at the clasp of the heavy chain belt around his waist.

The length of polished bicycle chain came loose. Coiling it round one fist, Mick swung it in small circles at chest level, and advanced once more.

Freaky jumped forwards, slashing the bottle in his hand sideways as he did so. The jagged edge plucked at Mick's sleeve, making a small gash in the leather of his jacket.

Irish Mick glanced down at the tear and let loose a bellow of anger.

'Right you bastard,' he spat viciously. 'Now you're really going to get it.'

With that he leapt forward, swinging the chain downwards in an arc towards Freaky's wrist. It coiled around his hand, smashing into his knuckles with such force that the remnants of the bottle smashed in his hand.

Freaky jumped back, screaming with pain and looked down at his open palm. It was pouring with blood where the glass had splintered into his fist. He shook his arm quickly, bespattering several onlookers with drops of blood.

Irish Mick cast the chain aside and moved forward.

'I can do this with my bare hands,' he muttered, and swung a fist at Freaky's face. The blow connected with a crunch, sending Freaky spinning back across the cafe to collapse across another table. He shook his head, jumped to his feet and picked up a chair in both hands. Like a lion tamer, he jabbed it forwards in defence as he closed in once again. Then, hurling it at Mick's head, he crouched low and went in for another head-butt.

Mick moved fast. Ducking to avoid the flying chair, he swung himself to one side as Freaky charged towards him like an onrushing bull. With all the skill of a matador, Mick let him rush almost past, then brought up one knee quickly. It caught Freaky in the chest, draining every bit of air out of his lungs. He went down in a heap to lay groaning and writhing with pain upon the floor.

Irish Mick looked down at him with hard, cold eyes, and stepped leisurely forwards to stand over him. The fight was over - it only remained for him to set the seal of Angel victory upon it. Drawing back one leg, he prepared to give the fallen Freaky a kick in the head with his heavy riding boot.

The noisy throb of a big hog engine distracted his attention. Irish Mick, along with everyone else, looked up towards the door. The front wheel of the bike mounted the kerb and crashed against the door, smashing it open like a battering ram. There was a stunned silence as hog and rider came through the door and into the cafe.

It was a grand entrance, a showstopper in the best theatrical tradition. Elaine had calculated it for maximum effect - and she had gained her objective. After the excitement and tension of the fight, her sudden appearance in such an unusual manner had every eye fixed upon her.

It was a stunning sight. Bernie had done his work well...the big Harley had never looked so good. It looked massive, incredibly powerful and aggressive in its new coat of matt black paint, and the chromium glittered and gleamed with the reflections of the lights inside the cafe.

Elaine too was transformed. She had always been a beautiful girl, and always looked cool, and self-assured. With the big hog under her, she seemed to have gained both in beauty and stature. The black leather suit had been polished until it gleamed, and worked carefully into the material were polished steel studs which spelled out the Angel name she had chosen for herself.

Big Mama.

She sat quietly on the hog, her eyes slowly but surely running round the cafe and appraising everybody present. The hog ticked over gently, shivering in time with its little song of repressed power. Elaine looked aloof, slightly mocking. A grim little smile played about her beautiful mouth and her head was thrown back with defiant pride. She knew how stunning she looked, and she knew the Harley-Davidson complemented her.

The masculine virility of the big hog was between her legs - the symbolism effective even to a person who couldn't understand it. Together, Elaine and the Harley completed a cypher - a secret message which screamed out blatant sexuality and the power that it brings. Elaine was a picture of sexual perfection, yet somehow above it...a fantasy-like figure shrouded in her own, very special, mystique. She was the Amazon Queen, the towering matriarchal figure of the Goddess Kali. And, like Kali, she wanted to control the minds and bodies of her Thug executioners.

Her lips curled gently into a faint sneer as she glanced down at the prone figure of Freaky.

'Haven't you anything better to do than fight amongst yourselves?' she questioned. 'You're Angels, or you're supposed to be. Angels fight citizens, they fight the system.'

13

She paused, letting the venom of her words sink in. Her gaze passed coldly over everyone. Many Angels avoided her eyes, instead gazing down sheepishly at the floor. Those who faced her gaze direct saw the flickering fire in her blue eyes, were hypnotised by it and eventually set in flame by it. They were converted instantly, bound to her immediately by some strange, instinctive sense.

Big Mama had arrived. The Hells Angels once again had a leader.

Danny the Deathlover was one of the last to capitulate. At his first sight of Elaine, a wave of shame and embarrassment had swept over him, forcing him to avoid her gaze. He remembered well the night when Marty had ordered him to rape her...the night when this girl had been cruelly beaten up and despoiled by five Hells Angels. He glanced down at Freaky, then at Irish Mick and saw the same shame in their eyes. Others who had been present on that fateful night remembered too, but gradually remembered also that Chopper had died, their leader had been taken from them. Now, somehow, they realised that they were being offered a chance to set the record straight, pull together once again.

Danny stepped forward slowly, approaching Elaine with something very much like a sense of reverence. He stared into her eyes.

'No hard feelings, huh?' he mumbled.

For a second, a strange faraway look flitted across Elaine's eyes as she remembered...

Then it was passed and gone. A faint smile crept across her face.

'No hard feelings, Danny,' she said simply.

Danny clicked his heels together sharply and performed a clenched-fist salute.

'We're with you...Mama,' he vowed in a soft voice.

He spoke for everyone.

CHAPTER FOUR

RUMBLE

Mama bent down and held out her hand to Freaky, who still lay on the floor.

'Get up, you dumb bastard,' she muttered with the faintest trace of humour in her voice.

Freaky scrambled to his feet groggily.

'You're out of practice, Freak,' she went on. 'I've seen better action in a school playground.'

Freaky grinned stupidly and looked suitably chastised.

'My heart wasn't really in it,' he mumbled by way of explanation.

Elaine nodded knowingly.

'Yeah,' she murmured reflectively. 'We ought to do something about that.'

Danny the Deathlover sprang forward eagerly.

'How's about some action tonight, Mama?' he asked excitedly.

A chorus of assent rippled round the cafe as the other Angels caught on to the new atmosphere of vitality.

'OK,' snapped Elaine quickly. 'We'll go and get some fist practice over in Bethnal Green. The Suedeheads will do for punch-bags.'

She eased the hog backwards through the door, swung it round and gunned the engine into a brief roar of screaming power. It was like a battle-call.

The cafe emptied out quickly, leaving a still-shaken Nick to clear up the debris and philosophise about the ups and downs of business. Outside, the Angels rapidly mounted their hogs and cracked the night air open with their declarations of war.

Big Mama streaked ahead of them, her golden hair fluttering behind her like a pennant. She pulled the Harley round every corner much tighter than necessary, revved the engine at each and every opportunity and pulled back the throttle every time there was more than ten yards of clear road. She was still on trial and she realised it...she would have to show class over and above that of any man.

Behind, Danny the Deathlover led the main party, his critical eyes upon the lone figure ahead and his mind surging with a new sense of pride.

...So they would be the only chapter with a female leader.

15

So what?

There might be criticism, even abuse. But they would have a unique status symbol, a strong sense of personal pride and identity. Danny smiled grimly as he thought of Elaine as a woman - a damned beautiful woman. There could be tricky times ahead - Danny was smart enough to realise that...but he also knew that he would always be right behind her, right there when he was needed. If Big Mama was to be a figurehead, then he, Danny, would be the warlord. With that combination, they could reign supreme.

Ahead, Elaine brought the big Harley to a sudden, screaming halt, flashily twisting the handlebars so that the rear wheel jumped and spun noisily against the tarmac. Danny grinned knowingly. She had learned the trick from Marty - and learned it well. It took a lot of skill to do it without having the hog skid away from underneath its rider.

He waved the rest of the gang down and slowly pulled alongside her.

'What's on?' he asked quietly.

Elaine gestured with one thumb towards a cinema further up the road.

'Reckon we'd do all right waiting for that lot to turn out,' she answered, glancing down at her watch.

Danny nodded in agreement.

'Yeah - that makes sense.'

'OK then. Tell the fellers to stow their hogs round the back somewhere and we'll go and wait in the boozer.' Elaine pointed across the road to a nearby pub.

Danny wheeled his hog round in the road and streaked back to the main bunch to pass on the orders. The Angels obediently peeled off in twos and threes to find places to hide their hogs, and then swaggered towards the pub.

It was packed out with the usual Saturday night crowd as they strolled into the saloon bar. The bar was three deep with people waiting to be served, and two brassy-looking barmaids dispensed drinks in their own good time. In one corner, on a tiny stage, a bored DJ played records and two even more bored go-go dancers twitched in vague time to the music.

Elaine watched the looks on the customers' faces carefully,

noting the usual reaction to an Angel invasion. Firstly, they registered surprise, then distaste...and eventually there was the unmistakable look of fear. Elaine beamed with pride and satisfaction.

Danny, Freaky and Irish Mick jostled their way through the crowd towards the bar. Anyone in the way was shoved roughly aside. Those who resented the treatment cast a wary look around, made a mental count of numbers, and swallowed their anger.

'All right darlin',' shouted Danny to the nearest barmaid. 'Just start pulling pints and stop when I call enough.'

The barmaid gave him a chilling look and made to walk off.

Danny's hand snaked over the counter to grasp her arm.

'I mean now, sweetheart,' he said menacingly. The girl shrugged off his grip with a quick gesture and headed for the beer tap. She took a fistful of pint mugs from the shelf and started to fill them.

Elaine called across the room.

'Hey, Danny - get me a scotch...double.'

She turned to Pretty Boy Parritt.

'Pretty, get over there by the window and keep a lookout on that cinema,' she ordered. He did as he was told.

She waved an arm at the rest of the Angels.

'Come on - get over here and clear a bit of breathing space.'

The whole gang surged forward slowly towards her, using their elbows and shoulders to push people out of the way. If a foot stayed too still for too long, the crunch of a heavy boot soon got it moving. Within seconds, the Angels had cleared a gap around themselves.

'That's better,' said Elaine with a sigh of relief. 'Now we can drink in peace.'

Danny returned with the first batch of drinks, handing out foaming pints of bitter to eager, clutching hands. He passed the scotch to Elaine, who took it, raised it to her lips and drained it in one gulp.

'Thanks Danny,' she said, handing him back the empty glass. 'Get me a refill, will ya?'

Danny smiled proudly and called out to Irish, who was still at the bar.

'Here Man. Mama wants this topped up.' He threw the whisky glass high above the crowd.

Irish Mick made only a half-hearted attempt to catch the glass. It sailed over the counter, to splinter against a row of bottles by the till.

Only the disc jockey was still making any sound at all. The go-go dancers paused in their gyrations as a hush fell across the pub.

Trouble was a definite smell in the air. It could almost be grabbed in handfuls, it was so thick.

The Angels had been too quiet for too long. Five weeks of doing nothing had festered inside their rebellious natures like pus under a scab. Now the scab was being torn off, to let the thick yellow matter underneath erupt out.

Elaine was high as a kite on her new-found power - plus a handful of Methedrine tablets she had taken before setting out. She didn't really need the extra stimulus of alcohol. Accepting her new double whisky, she downed it in one and dropped the glass to the floor.

She walked slowly towards the stage, pushing everyone out of the way. The disc-jockey kept playing his records, hoping that the tension would pass. The go-go dancers had recovered themselves slightly and were moving sensuously but warily.

Elaine cleared the last few feet in front of the stage and took a flying leap. She landed between the two dancers, and quickly shouldered them off the stage roughly.

'Get them scrubbers out of here,' she screamed at the top of her voice. 'I'll show you what a real dance looks like.'

A pulsing, sexy Reggae record was playing. Elaine caught the beat and started to shake her hips in perfect time. Her whole body came alive - writhing, weaving and snaking about the small stage with the rhythm. Her hands played down the front of her costume, slipped slowly across down over her prominent breasts to join together in the region of her crotch. She pressed them against herself, jerking her pelvis outwards in blatant, obscene gestures of sexuality. She reached up again, fingering with the silver zipper and pulling it down to her waist. She leant over forwards, shaking her torso from side to side so that her free breasts jiggled from side to side.

The record came to an end.

There was a silence.

Elaine looked up at the DJ with a wicked smile.

'Come on, man...let's have something really hot,' she muttered.

The DJ didn't answer her. Instead, he carefully replaced the pick-up arm in its rest and sat back in his chair.

'There'll be no more music until you clear off the stage,' he threatened.

Elaine threw him a long, cool stare.

'Wanna bet?' she asked grimly. Her eyes flickered across the pub towards the bar. Already, sensing trouble, the Angels had started to move menacingly towards the stage.

'If you know what's good for you - you'll get some music on that turntable...fast.' hissed Elaine quietly. The DJ glanced at the approaching mob, thought for a second, then hastily slipped a record on the turntable. The amplified blare of pop music echoed around the room once again.

Elaine had tired of dancing. She jumped off the stage just as Irish Mick and Freaky approached it. Freaky grinned stupidly up at the empty stage, finished his beer and slammed the empty glass down on a nearby table. He took a running jump at the stage and stood up.

'Don't like that record,' he complained to the DJ, strolling towards him. To emphasise his words, Freaky snatched at the delicate pick-up arm, sending it streaking across the playing record with an angry screech.

The DJ jumped to his feet angrily.

'You stupid bastard,' he spat viciously. 'There's two hundred quid's worth of equipment here.' He placed his hand in the middle of Freaky's chest and pushed hard.

He staggered backwards, lost his footing on the edge of the stage and crashed to the floor in a heap. Freaky climbed to his feet slowly, dusting himself down.

'That,' he muttered nastily, 'was a very silly thing to do.'

Freaky didn't have to call for help. Suddenly, everyone was right there by his side...with one thought in their minds. A fellow Angel had been assaulted. Revenge was called for.

Half a dozen Angels clambered onto the stage.

Freaky reached down and lifted up one of the heavy stereo

loudspeakers.

'Two hundred quid's worth, eh?' he muttered slowly. 'Well this ought to take care of a tenner's worth.' He smashed the speaker cabinet to the floor.

Irish Mick turned his attention to the amplifiers. Seizing handfuls of electrical cable, he tugged on them viciously, pulling out plugs and snapping delicate wiring connections. The music ceased abruptly.

Freaky finished off the job on the loudspeaker, crashing his booted foot down on it so that the wooden cabinet splintered and cracked open. Danny the Deathlover roughly shoved the terror-stricken DJ aside and wrenched the pick-up arm away from the record deck. He threw it casually into one corner of the room.

The DJ was screaming now at the top of his voice.

'Call the police. For Christ's sake someone call the police.'

Above the din, Pretty Boy Parritt's voice rang out from across the pub.

'The cinema's turning out now.'

Elaine waved one hand at Danny and Freaky, who were just about to teach the DJ a more physical lesson.

'Come on - let's split,' she called.

Danny turned towards her, then looked back at the wrecked equipment ruefully. He bent down, picked up the other speaker and hurled it against the wall as an afterthought.

They followed Elaine out of the pub obediently, standing outside the door in a mob.

Across the road, the Saturday-night crowd poured out of the cinema in small groups. Elaine watched intently as the middle-aged couples on their one night a week outing trickled through the doors and set off for the comfort of their semi-detached homes. She ignored them, along with the younger couples who strolled out arm-in-arm and cuddled their way to the nearest fish and chip shop.

At last, she saw what she was looking for.

A small group of suedeheads, dressed in their imitation crombie overcoats and their best Saturday night finery. There were about eight of them - six boys and a couple of young girls.

Elaine pulled Danny the Deathlover by the sleeve and pointed over at them.

'There's our target practice,' she muttered. 'We'll see which way they're going before we go and get the hogs.'

They watched carefully as the kids turned left outside the cinema and strolled casually down the road. Three of them stopped for a while outside a clothing store to do a bit of window shopping, then the main bunch turned a corner into a side road.

'OK,' snapped Elaine. 'Let's go and get 'em.'

She broke off and ran for her hog, parked just around the corner.

Once more, the roar of motorcycle engines shuddered through the night air as the Angels banded together like a wolf pack in search of prey. They drove slowly down the road until they came to the side street.

Elaine looked all around carefully, noting another road which seemed to run parallel.

'Danny...take a couple of boys and go up that way,' she ordered. 'Cut 'em off at the next junction. We'll follow them up here.'

She waved to the rest of the gang behind her and eased the Harley away from the kerb with the engine throbbing gently. Danny took Pretty Boy Parritt and a few others and streaked off at a tangent.

The suedehead kids weren't expecting any 'bovver'. As far as they were concerned, this was a quiet, peaceful Saturday night.

Their first intimation of impending trouble was the low, melodic throbbing of two dozen motorcycle engines. Turning in the direction of the noise they saw the Angels cruising slowly up the road towards them. Their reaction was immediate and spontaneous. They ran.

They scattered across the road, leaving their girls to fend for themselves.

Elaine accelerated, quickly closing the gap between her and the two girls, who stood still, slightly bewildered. Elaine reached out almost casually, and snatched each girl's handbag in turn. Hanging the captured booty on her handlebars, she rode off again, leaving the surprised girls to shout obscenities after her.

The suedeheads kept running - straight up the road towards the corner junction. They were almost there when they saw their reception committee.

Danny and his boys had dismounted, and stood spaced across

the width of the road. Heavy steel chains swung from each wrist.

The suedeheads stopped, and looked back at the bigger party of Angels pursuing them. They looked back quickly at Danny and his boys and rapidly took the only course open to them.

They raced forward, hoping to break though the cordon and make a run for it.

Behind them, the Angels pulled back on their throttles and quickly closed in for the kill. Danny the Deathlover flicked quick signals to his companions and fixed his eyes firmly upon the leading kid running towards him. The kid ran straight for Danny, jumping sideways at the last instant in an attempt to get straight through without a fight. He didn't quite make it. Danny's foot snaked out quickly, catching the kid under the shins and sending him crashing to the pavement. Danny kicked him once in the ribs to keep him still and turned to engage the next fugitive.

The suedeheads were trapped - and they knew it. The vastly different odds left them with no hope of scrapping their way out of trouble. Almost resignedly, they each chose a partner in combat and moved in for the inevitable punch-up.

It wasn't a fight. It was slaughter.

Two of the kids got smart and fell to the ground after a couple of punches from Freaky and Irish Mick. They went down - and stayed down, knowing full well that the worst they could expect was a few boots smashing into their bodies.

The rest of the kids put up at least a token attempt at retaliation, but were soon overpowered.

Each suedehead was held firmly by two Angels and slammed up against the nearest wall.

'OK. Freaky...Mick,' called out Elaine. 'Now's your chance to get in a bit of that sparring practice you need.'

Freaky laughed and chose a victim at random.

Like a punch-drunk boxer releasing his venom on a punchbag, he pounded blow after blow into the defenceless kid's body. After slamming away for half a minute or so, he shrugged, drew back and poised himself for the final blow.

The kid screamed as he saw it coming - a scream which was abruptly cut short as Freaky's gloved fist smashed into the bridge of his nose and cut up and across his eyes. His head snapped backwards with a sharp cracking sound and lolled sideways. The two Angels holding his arms let go, and the kid slithered to the ground unconscious, blood pouring from his nose.

Elaine stepped up to inspect the damage. She looked down on the suedehead dispassionately for a second, then turned to Freaky and smiled.

'That's better, Freak,' she murmured happily. 'That's more like it.'

She bent down beside the kid and started to fish through his pockets.

'Watcha doing, Mama?' asked Freaky curiously.

Elaine pulled out the kid's wallet and carelessly rifled its contents. Extracting a thin bundle of notes, she screwed them up in her hand and stuffed them down the front of her leather suit.

'Got a debt to settle with Bernie,' she explained, and threw the empty wallet into the gutter.

She looked round. Only one kid remained on his feet, putting up a reasonable show by trading blow for blow with three Angels.

'Finish him off,' shouted Elaine to two more Angels who were waiting about aimlessly. They closed in to make the odds five to one and quickly dropped the kid to his knees. A boot in his face put him down for good.

The gang rested from their labours - looking round contentedly at the six beaten suedeheads grovelling on the ground.

'Go through their pockets,' snapped Elaine. 'I want every bit of loose change they're carrying...and take off any watches and rings.'

Danny the Deathlover looked at her in surprise for a moment, noticing the quick glances which were exchanged between many of the Angels. This wasn't just a simple gang-fight...this was organised robbery.

'From now on, we're collecting funds for charity,' said Elaine by way of explanation. 'So make sure everyone gives generously.'

Danny paused for one more brief moment before nodding to Freaky and Pretty Boy. 'OK,' he snapped. 'Strip 'em.'

Pretty Boy and Freaky quickly cleaned out the pockets of the suedeheads and collected the booty together.

'OK...stuff it in your pockets and let's get the hell out of here,' grinned Elaine, striding back to her hog and remounting. She kicked the engine into life and whipped the big Harley round in a tight circle. She roared off without waiting for the rest of the Angels to remount.

Back in the Greek's, Big Mama presided over the counting of the spoils. The coins and notes mounted up upon one of Nick's grubby tables and Freaky and Mick emptied their pockets.

It wasn't a bad haul, reflected Elaine happily. The contents of the two stolen handbags had been disappointing - yielding only a couple of quid in loose cash and a few bits and pieces of cheap chain-store make-up.

...But the boys were a different matter. They liked to carry a few quid with them to flash around...and Friday had been payday. From the suedeheads, the Angels had gathered a grand total of sixty-eight quid, two watches and three gas lighters. Elaine didn't bother to remind anyone about the fifteen quid tucked down the front of her suit. That was earmarked for Bernie...for services rendered.

She scooped the money off the table, after making sure that most of the Angels had counted it. Picking up one pound note, she folded it carefully into the shape of a paper dart and threw it across the cafe towards the serving counter.

'Here, Nick...give us all coffees,' she called, as the note sailed past the counter and landed in the sinkful of greasy dishes.

Elaine held the rest of the money in her fist and brandished it in the air.

'This goes straight into the community fund...OK?' she asked. The Angels nodded in assent. Mama seemed to know what she was doing.

'This bread is here for all of us,' Elaine went on. 'We'll keep adding to it until we've got a real treasury department. If any of you have repair bills you can't afford...you can come to me and borrow. If you need money for anything - it'll be here for the asking. If anyone gets busted by the fuzz...we've got the bread for the bail and to pay fines. When we want a party...the booze is taken care of .'

Irish Mick leaned over the table and picked up one of the watches.

'What about this stuff?'

Elaine shrugged. 'We fence it off to someone who doesn't ask too many questions,' she said casually.

'I know a bent jeweller who might be interested,' put in a tall blonde-haired Angel named Adolph. 'He deals with all sorts of stuff...provided it ain't too hot.'

'Is he safe?' Elaine queried.

Adolph grinned hugely. 'Safe as bleedin' houses,' he avowed. 'He's me bruvver.'

A roar of laughter bubbled round the group. Elaine scooped up the watches and lighters and handed them to Adolph.

'Here you are...see what he'll do with these - and tell him there can be more if the price is right.'

Adolph slipped the merchandise into his pocket. 'I'll do it ter-morrer,' he vowed.

Danny the Deathlover leaned across the table to Elaine.

'Looks like you've got plans,' he whispered quietly.

Elaine smiled wryly back at him.

'Big plans, Danny,' she replied softly. 'But first, we've really got to get things organised. First thing tomorrow, I want you to start putting the word around that this chapter is expanding. Any riders who've dropped out recently...I want them in here next Saturday night. Any small groups with no recognised leader...I want 'em. Lone riders, if they're tough enough we'll initiate 'em. I want everybody who's got the guts to be a Hells Angel to be in this place with their colours flying.'

Danny smiled with a distant, dreamlike happiness. Elaine's enthusiasm was contagious.

'Yeah...I'll see to it, Mama,' he said firmly. Then, as an afterthought.

'Chopper would've liked that,' he added.

CHAPTER FIVE

SUPERSPADE

The Greek's wasn't big enough to contain the crowd who turned up faithfully on Saturday night. They sat and stood around from wall to wall, huddled in corners and spilled out of the door into the street outside.

That was at nine o'clock. By ten, they were still coming in droves - curious to find out about Big Mama and eager to bask in the reflected power of their own massed numbers.

Elaine looked round proudly and tried to count heads. It was an impossible task. Suddenly it seemed as though everyone between the ages of sixteen and thirty in the city of London was a Hells Angel. Elaine nodded, with curt, royalty-like gestures at those faces she recognised...glanced carefully and summed up those she didn't.

Small, leaderless chapters clung together in tight little bunches; lone riders hovered in the background, backs against the nearest wall so no one could see the unadorned backs of their denim overjackets.

Elaine noticed Ethel, the chapter leader from Dagenham and most of his small band. There was Frenchy, Grass, Mudso and Trucker, Pee Wee and the small Italian-looking boy they called Sam the Spick. Even Ethel had gathered a few new faces...young bloods whose faces all bore the common distinguishing mark of violence.

The girls huddled together in one corner of the cafe, seeking comfort in their own kind and flashing looks of envy, curiosity and wonderment at the strange and supreme queen who had appeared to rule their menfolk. Even the mamas and the old ladies joined them, creating a small flock of females who lived up to their nickname of sheep.

Outside, the occasional growl of hog engines announced the arrival of new riders to swell the horde. The atmosphere was tense and expectant: old enmities were forgotten and past rivalries ignored temporarily. There was a strange spirit of camaraderie binding everyone together...a spirit which seemed to centre on the slim, black-suited figure in the centre of the room.

Danny the Deathlover was never far away from her side. He patrolled around her, strutting proudly like a peacock and glaring in defiance at anyone who dared to cast a critical eye. He had cast himself well in the role of protector and first lieutenant.

Nick the Greek watched everything with a sense of foreboding. His florid, impassive face housed a pair of eyes which saw many things, but reflected little. His mind formed vague and ill-defined opinions which never seemed to crystallise into any firm beliefs. In the Hells Angels, he had no great faith, yet on the other hand he stubbornly refused to even attempt to resist them. One moment he saw them as a bunch of high-spirited kids, the next as an organised gang of dangerous hoodlums. Nick never quite made up his mind...he merely observed, recorded the information and then studiously ignored it.

He was aware, however, that a subtle change was taking place before his eyes. He sensed the birth, or rebirth, of a movement...a philosophy and way of life which would turn, inevitably, into a cult of power.

...And power, as Nick knew well from his home country, gave birth to evil and corruption.

Elaine saw only a dream materialising in front of her. She moved forward unconsciously, almost innocently as the driving force which had been born in her took control.

...And in the recesses of her mind, the ghost of Chopper Harris walked abroad with a smiling face and eyes which burned with the gleam of achievement.

Only a few stragglers arrived outside the cafe now. It was time to take control, start the delicate business of moulding together groups of people who were by their very nature dedicated to rebellion against organisation.

Yet this one common factor could be the unifying element, Elaine realised shrewdly. Just as Adolph Hitler had united his people against a common scapegoat, so she could manipulate a rabble into an army with common ideals and shared victories.

She pushed her way through the crowd towards the serving counter, producing a rolled sheet of paper from beneath her costume.

Taking four drawing pins from her pocket, she pinned the sheet carefully to the side of the counter and turned to face her audience.

'OK. Let's start talking business,' she shouted stridently across the cafe. The babble of conversation died away as all eyes turned to face her.

Elaine paused for effect as the crowded cafe became deathly quiet. A small area cleared around her as the Angels shuffled backwards to give her a little room.

When she spoke, her voice was calm, yet powerful.

'You're all probably wondering why we are all here tonight,' she started.

A tiny ripple of conversation broke out and trembled round the room. It ceased as soon as it had started, and Elaine continued.

'First of all, we are here because we are all Hells Angels,' she said simply. 'So perhaps it might be as well for me to remind you all exactly what that means.

'Out there'...she gestured theatrically towards the door... 'are the citizens - the pigs. We're different. We're out on our own because that's the way we want to be, and the way we have to be. We're different to them and we're better than them...but never forget one thing...there's more of them than there are of us...and for that reason alone, we have to stick together.'

Mama paused to glance around the cafe, making sure her words were sinking in. Fostering the correct attitude of group identity was the first important step. She smiled inwardly at the blur of attentive faces. So far it was working well.

'Don't a single one of you ever forget the importance of that sticking together.' she went on. 'It's our protection from harassment by the fuzz and by the citizens. It's our safety net against bother from anything from suedeheads to Pakis...and most of all it gives us a code to follow and a reminder of everything we stand for.'

Murmurs of approval rippled round the cafe. Chapter leaders started to push their way through the crowd towards the front.

Elaine motioned to Danny the Deathlover, who stood on her left-hand side. He drew himself up to his full height, puffing his chest out with pride. He cleared his throat.

'Mama's telling you that there's gonna have to be some changes made,' he started off. 'A lot of the smaller chapters have been splitting up recently, and we ain't got no central committee for sorting out anybody who gets out of line. There's also been a lot of in-fighting between groups, and this don't do any of us any good. Now Mama's got some damned good plans here, and we could have this whole goddamned city eating out of our hands if we do as she says...so I want you all to listen to her good.'

He moved sideways, giving Elaine the floor. She turned to the diagram pinned to the counter and pointed at the roughly-drawn 'family tree' of Angel leadership.

'This is a pattern,' she said clearly. 'It's based on the American system...and we might as well all remember that the Hells Angels originated in the States and we started out by following their lead.'

Her finger pointed towards the central symbol in the diagram. It was like a circle, the hub of a hog wheel, and spokes radiated out from it to smaller circles.

'This is the central co-ordinating committee,' said Elaine. 'Here we have the treasury, the bail-bond scheme and the armoury.'

A voice interrupted gruffly. It was Ethel, from Dagenham. He stepped forward to the front.

'Who's on this committee?' he asked sarcastically. '...Besides you and Danny, that it?'

Elaine stared at him coolly for a second or so.

'You, maybe...if you earn your place,' she replied calmly. 'The Hells Angels are a democratic institution. The committee will be made up of chosen chapter leaders and anyone else who is put there by majority vote. Any more questions?' she finished, looking Ethel directly in the eyes.

'OK,' he grunted, and shuffled back a couple of steps.

'So,' Elaine went on. 'The central committee meets regularly to make sure everything runs smoothly. All major decisions on runs, policy matters and territorial rights are made here. The results feed out from the committee to the individual chapters...'

Her finger traced one of the spokes out of one of the smaller circles on the diagram.

'...And the chapter leaders pass on information to all members. The system works just the same in reverse...any personal bothers are passed through the chapter leader to the central body.

'...Any more questions?' she finished.

'What's with this Treasury bit?' Sam the Spick wanted to know.

'Every chapter will be responsible for collecting their fair share of bread,' Elaine explained. 'How they do it, we don't mind...it can be from subscriptions, initiation fees to new recruits or spoils gathered on raids. We've got a good fence who can dispose of stolen jewellery, watches, cameras...any stuff like that. Bernie will handle any stolen hogs which are a bit too hot. As far as the Treasury is concerned, books will be kept and any chapter leader can check them anytime he wants. The money will be used for anyone in trouble, or for financing runs, parties, or any other Angel activities.'

Mama finished her speech and beckoned once more to Danny the Deathlover. He took up the speaker's position proudly.

'Right then. Now you've all got the picture,' he said, affecting his usual pseudo-American turn of phrase. 'Next off, we gotta do something about all the stragglers who don't belong to an official chapter. They'd all better start looking around for the nearest chapter and get solid...fast. Anybody who hasn't turned out yet better start making some contact with any chapter who's willing to take you.'

'OK Man. You got one for a start,' said a voice from the doorway. Danny looked up as a tall, lithe negro youth pushed his way through the crowd.

'How about me...I wanna turn out for your chapter,' he said, in a challenging voice.

There was an angry buzz of disapproval at once.

Pretty Boy Parritt put it into words.

'We don't have no bloody coons in the Angels,' he spat out viciously. A chorus of agreement followed his words.

The negro kid didn't turn a hair.

'Who says?' he challenged aggressively. 'There's black members in the States.'

Pretty Boy stepped forward menacingly to add some physical impact to his words.

'Hold it, Pretty,' Elaine shouted curtly. 'He's right.'

She turned towards the newcomer.

'What's your name?' she asked bluntly.

'Winston. Winston Oliver.'

Elaine beckoned him up to the front. He pushed his way through the large crowd.

'What hog you got?' asked Elaine, putting the all-important question first.

The kid grinned proudly.

'Norton Commando,' he said. 'Two months old and like a bird.'

Elaine pursed her lips and nodded her head approvingly. The Commando was a highly prized hog...a 750cc power-pack of screaming fury which could race from a standing start to 60mph in four and a half seconds, with just four more seconds to bust the ton.

'Can you use it?' Elaine asked with a grim smile.

'Try me,' shot back Winston.

Elaine stared at him piercingly for a few seconds.

'That's exactly what we're going to do...right now,' she answered, and gestured towards the door.

'Let's go see, shall we?'

With joyous whoops and war-cries, the Angel horde emptied itself into the street, sweeping Winston along with it.

Outside, he turned to Elaine and spoke quietly.

'She's round the corner...I'll go get her,' he muttered, and walked slowly off.

A few seconds later, an ear-splitting roar of power announced that he had kicked the machine into life. He came round the corner with a squeal of tortured tyres.

It was a beautiful hog. The body work was bright orange, with sleek black upholstery and gleaming chrome everywhere. The high handlebars and lack of mudguards showed that it was an outlaw cycle and not just a common garbage wagon.

Winston sat astride the throbbing hog with defiant pride.

'You want to find out what I can do,' he hissed quietly. '...Then let me see six of you with enough guts to really find out.'

Danny the Deathlover looked at him uncertainly.

'What you planning to do, Man?' he asked.

Winston grinned widely, showing a huge flash of white teeth in his black face.

'Ain't you got the guts to find out?' he questioned back.

Danny couldn't evade the direct challenge to his class.

'I've got the guts for anything,' he snapped back. 'You just give the word...boy.'

'OK,' said Winston. 'Then all I need is five more brave boys just like you.'

'Any volunteers,' called Danny, looking at the assembled crowd.

31

There was a noticeable pause before Ethel, Grass, Irish Mick, Freaky and Max the Knife stepped slowly forward.

'OK fellers...let's have some fun,' said Winston with a grin, and slowly cruised out into the middle of the street.

He ran down the road for about fifty yards and waited for the six to catch him up.

'The first two stand right here,' he said. 'One each side of the handlebars.'

Irish Mick and Max the Knife stood themselves a couple of feet away from each side of the Norton.

'Close in a little fellers,' Winston sneered. 'You think I got the plague or something?'

The two Angels inched forward until each stood only six inches from the protruding end of the handlebars.

'OK...now you just stay quiet as a couple of mice,' said Winston, and moved his hog another ten yards up the road.

'Let's make this a bit more interesting,' he said with an evil laugh as he stopped once again. He moved over to the side of the road, only a foot from the pavement.

Danny the Deathlover and Freaky took up their positions as Winston cruised another fifteen yards up the road. This time he pulled into the centre again and let the last two Angels take up their positions.

As soon as they were still, he yanked back his throttle and roared off up the road. Seventy-five yards farther on, he swung the hog round in a circle and snapped on his headlight.

There was a breathless hush as everyone present suddenly realised what he was going to do. They waited expectantly.

The Norton snarled into life with a scream of fury and launched itself down the road towards the assembled crowd...and the six human nine-pins.

The way he had positioned them, Winston didn't even have a straight line to aim at. Once through the first pair, he had a curve to where Danny and Freaky stood at the side of the road, and then just a few yards to straighten up and head for the six-inch gap which Max and Irish Mick had between them and annihilation.

The headlight was totally blinding as the Norton screamed down the road towards the quaking victims. Maybe they would have chosen to run...but there wasn't really that much time.

At a screaming seventy miles an hour, Winston flashed between Ethel and Grass, swung the hog over to slice through Danny and Freaky and blasted on through the last pair.

There was an unearthly scream as he flashed past Irish Mick and Max the Knife. Winston slammed on the brakes, bringing the Norton to a slithering halt.

'Jesus Christ!' shouted Max, who had given vent to the scream. 'I felt the bastard...I actually felt the mother-fugger touch me.'

Suddenly, a wave of relieved laughter swept through the group as Max ran to the lights of Nick's cafe to inspect his jacket.

There, at waist level, was the frightening evidence.

...A long, jagged tear where one of Winston's handlebars had pulled at the cloth, ripping it away from the button and shredding the flimsy demin material.

'My originals,' screamed Max in fury. 'The swine's torn my originals.' He didn't have to add that one inch more would have sent his innards sluicing to the ground in a bloody mess.

Winston cruised back up the street, switched off his engine and parked the hog. Dismounting, he swaggered up to Elaine.

'Well?' he said flatly. 'Good enough for an Angel?'

Elaine smiled calmly. The guy had shown real class, but she didn't want to betray it.

'Not bad,' she muttered grudgingly. 'I've seen worse.'

She nodded over to Pretty Boy Parritt, who hurried towards her.

'You voiced the first objection,' she pointed out to him. 'Winston here wants to show us how he can handle himself in a bundle.'

Winston was already preparing himself by peeling off his black leather jerkin. He didn't have to be told that the second important test had to be taken. Any would-be Hells Angel had to show his class in riding skill...and his ability to participate. It was all part of the initiation ceremony.

Elaine called over to Max the Knife.

'Max...that guy ripped your jacket...so you've got a grudge,' she snapped. Then, turning to the crowd... 'One more guy who wants to get some exercise.'

Grass stepped forward eagerly.

'That crazy bastard scared the shit out of me,' he said with a

33

nervous laugh. 'I reckon I owe him something for that.'

'OK,' snapped Elaine. 'In your own time...no blades, chains or dusters...this one's a fair fight.'

It was a fair fight all right...by Angel standards. Three against one...the only way a novice Angel could prove himself and go through the necessary suffering at the same time.

Winston squared up for the ordeal...and the inevitable beating...ahead of him. He watched warily as his three opponents circled him, spreading out to surround him completely.

Pretty Boy Parritt rushed in first, swinging a low jab to the belly.

It never connected. Winston seemed to pivot on one foot like a ballet dancer. He was a foot away as Pretty Boy lunged past, carried on by his own impetus.

...But the gap wasn't enough to protect him from the point of Winston's boot, which snaked out to deliver a cracking blow upon his shin.

Winston whirled round as Grass rushed at him from behind. He stepped quickly aside, crouched down and held out one outstretched hand. It was flat, like a shovel...the classic karate position.

Grass didn't have a chance. The side of Winston's left hand sliced into his solar plexus with all the force of a trained judo scholar. He doubled up in pain, and crashed to his knees.

Max the Knife had been ready to attack, but he saw the danger and kept his distance. As Grass climbed, gasping, to his feet, he called out.

'We'll have to take the mother all together...he's a sharp cookie.' He circled warily, meeting up with Grass and Pretty Boy.

The three went in as one man.

Grass bent over, his bullet-like head aimed for the kid's belly. Max and Pretty Boy each headed for an arm, aiming to slam him into a full nelson. Only Pretty Boy managed to beat Winston's snake-like movement. Grasping him by the shoulder, he held the kid just long enough for Grass's head-butt to get through.

The force of the butt - well below the belt - would have winded most men, and put more than a few to the ground. Winston absorbed the shock with well-trained stomach muscles, and hardly flinched.

He was also quick enough to bring up his right knee under

Grass's face. There was a dull crack as chin made sudden contact with knee-bone.

Max the Knife was immediately behind the kid now, and he saw his chance. He slammed a vicious punch into Winston's kidneys, following it up with his knee jerking up quickly to give the kid a jarring blow in the base of the spine.

Grass picked himself up for the second time and took advantage of the kid's hurt. His huge, ham-like fist crunched into Winston's face, starting a thin trickle of blood running from above one eye.

The blow, although successful, was his last in that fight. As though incensed to the point of drawing some new, supernatural power, Winston shrugged free of Pretty Boy's hold on his arm, danced sideways and flashed upon Grass with both arms flailing like demented windmills.

With a jab to the throat, a blow on the side of the ear and a chop on the back of the neck, he quickly despatched Grass. Unconscious, he slumped to the ground and stayed there.

The kid was tiring now and the superior numbers had to tell. Pretty Boy got another punch through to his face, smearing the blood which was already coursing down the side of his nose and into his mouth. He received a stinging slash across the eyes for his trouble, but the kid was finished. Max the Knife slammed three punches into his kidneys and turned his attention to the kid's stomach.

Winston sank slowly to his knees as blows rained into his abdomen. As he sprawled to the ground, Pretty Boy drew back his foot to boot him in the teeth.

Max laid a restraining arm upon his shoulder and pulled him back sharply.

'Let him be,' he muttered. 'The kid's had enough...and he put up a bloody good fight.'

He reached down and pulled Winston to his feet. He was smiling.

Max held out his hand in friendship. Winston looked at him quizzically for a second, then a painful smile spread across his black face. He wiped the blood from his face with the back of his left hand and took Max's firmly in his right. They shook hands with a gesture which bespoke a long and lasting friendship.

Grass recovered consciousness, and staggered to his feet groggily. He was just in time to see Pretty Boy Parritt grudgingly slap Winston on the back in congratulation.

Grass stumbled forwards and held out a shaking, trembling hand.

'There ain't many men who can put me down,' he muttered. 'But when I meet one...I sure as hell respect him for it.'

The two shook hands formally.

Elaine stepped forwards and stood directly in front of Winston.

'You put up a damned good show,' she admitted. 'Where did you learn all that fancy stuff?'

Winston grinned. 'I studied Oriental fighting arts for six years,' he said. 'I ain't exactly an expert...but it sure comes in useful sometimes.'

Elaine nodded thoughtfully.

'Your first job is gonna be teaching us all a few of those tricks,' she muttered.

Then, as an afterthought: 'Oh, that means you're in, by the way. You can turn out sometime next week...as soon as we baptise your originals.'

Winston's face beamed with pride and the realisation of a dream.

'Thanks, Mama,' he said humbly. 'I'll be a good Angel.'

'I'm sure you will,' responded Elaine. 'And by the way...we're going to christen you with the legal name of Superspade.'

Winston pursed his lips reflectively for a moment.

'Yeah...I like that,' he said at last, and his black face creased into a huge smile.

Elaine turned her back on him and moved back into the Greek's.

'Now we'd better start sorting out this committee,' she called.

The mob followed her inside.

CHAPTER SIX

THE WHARF RATS

From the outside, the clubhouse looked no different from any one of a dozen derelict warehouses along the banks of the long-abandoned canal. A fading, peeling sign above the frontal loading bay announced it as a furniture warehouse, but the company had been out of business for nearly six years. Once, the canal had run right through the borough of Islington, serving the hundreds of loaded barges which trafficked between the City of London and the busy railway centre at Kings Cross. Now, what had once been part of the proud Grand Union Canal was a sluggish, stagnant patch of muddy brown water, silted up with filth and sewerage and serving only as a watering place for countless thousands of rats.

Quite apart from the fact that it provided seclusion, the site had somehow seemed particularly appropriate to Mama. The owners of the abandoned old buildings waited patiently for the land and property value to soar upwards - hoped from week to week that some new development scheme would pass through the local Borough Council to make their fortunes overnight. Meanwhile, they were only too happy to let the crumbling warehouses on short-term rents to anyone who came along with hard cash.

...And they didn't ask too many questions.

Inside the vast warehouse, a few changes had been made, and the character of the Hells Angels was plainly evident in the haphazard decorations. The floor remained a bare expanse of concrete, with several old mattresses thrown down to serve as seating accommodation. On the uneven walls, several coats of blood-red paint served as a backdrop for the dozens of Nazi relics, odd motorcycle spare parts and souvenirs of raids which were nailed up at irregular intervals.

A huge SS flag dominated one wall, accompanied by crudely-drawn swastikas and witchcraft symbols. Several nude pin-ups cut from various magazines adorned other corners of the warehouse, and a poster depicting Che Guevara wearing a halo sat next to a colour picture of Peter Fonda in a scene from 'Easy Rider'.

Slogans and obscenities written in lipstick, blood and felt-tip pen filled up any available gaps.

Mama strolled alone through the empty clubhouse, carefully checking over the preparations for the big night's entertainment ahead. Dozens of beer crates were piled up in one corner, with enough booze to flood the entire building. In the centre of the floor, a huge pile of dirty old blankets and newspapers waited for the inevitable casualties who would crash out for the night.

Irish Mick's electrical genius had provided the wiring for the crudely-rigged stereo system which could flood the whole warehouse with sound. Loudspeakers cluttered up what had once been a loading dock and a tangled mess of wires clambered up the wall like poison ivy.

Mama walked slowly along the battery of oil heaters which lined one wall, checking each one in turn. Even with the heaters blasting on full power, the open expanse of the room was bitterly cold. It was, after all, late November, and the warehouse had never been entirely weatherproof.

Finally satisfied with the preparations, Mama sat down on one of the mattresses, lit a cigarette and lay back to reflect upon the immediate future.

It was now six weeks since the first committee meeting, and Mama felt a glow of pride in what she had achieved in that short space of time.

Most of the North London chapters were now consolidated under her direct command. They had the clubhouse, and the treasury was well stocked. Four pubs in the area were paying healthy sums in protection money to the Angels, and there were plenty more on the agenda.

It was a small, but significant start, Elaine reflected with a smile...but then even the Mafia had probably started out from humble beginnings.

Altogether, it was a good scene. The Hells Angels were no longer a rabble of wild ones on hogs...they were an organised force, a syndicate, a brotherhood.

...And tonight was party night - a time for celebrations and the gathering of clans. A time for all Angels to meet and rejoice in the celebration of their own rites and traditions.

Tonight would be a double celebration. The initiation of Superspade as an official Hells Angel, and to top off the evening, an Angel 'marriage' ceremony.

As she finished her cigarette and crushed the stub into the concrete floor, Mama heard the low growl of hog engines outside. Seconds later, Adolph and Freaky strolled in - each clutching a bottle of whisky.

'Hi, Mama,' they muttered in unison, and scrambled down on to a handy mattress.

Elaine nodded dumbly in acknowledgement. Freaky grinned and proffered the bottle. Taking the second nod of the head as a sign of assent, he hurled the bottle across the room towards her. Mama caught it adroitly and pulled the stopper out with her teeth. She took a long, deep pull at the firewater liquid.

'Everything OK?' asked Adolph.

'Great.'

Adolph glanced at the huge stock of drink.

'Looks fine that end,' he muttered happily, and uncorked his own bottle. 'Oh, by the way...'

He fished in his pocket and pulled out a grubby linen bag. Rising, he walked across to Mama and tipped the contents out in front of her. Three watches clattered to the stone floor.

'Me brother says he don't want to touch these,' he said apologetically. 'Says they've got inscriptions on 'em...means they can be traced too easily.'

Elaine glanced down at the watches and shrugged carelessly.

'What'd he give for the other stuff?' she asked casually.

'A pony,' replied Adolph equally casually, and peeled off a thin bundle of five-pound notes. '...And he says he could do with some more trannies.'

Mama scooped up the three watches in her hand and held them out towards Adolph and Freaky.

'Any good to either of you?' she asked.

Freaky shook his head, extending both wrists so that the wristwatch on both could be clearly seen.

'OK,' said Mama in a bored voice. Rising to her feet, she crossed the clubhouse to the small window which overlooked the canal. She flung the watches carelessly into the dirty water. There was no point in keeping hot merchandise hanging around. If their fence didn't want to take it, then it might as well be dumped. The rate that spoils of war were coming in, three miserable watches were chicken-feed.

'How many radios does he want?' she asked Adolph.

He shrugged. 'Many as you can get, I guess.'

Mama nodded thoughtfully.

'The record shop in Upper Street,' she murmured. 'We'll do it tomorrow night.'

That took care of the underworld's need for stolen transistor radios. Mama steered the conversation to other things.

'Seen Danny today?'

Freaky nodded.

'About an hour ago...said he'd be along with the Dagenham boys about eight,' he said. 'They're going down to pick up some hash at Rotherhithe.'

Mama glanced at her watch. It was four-fifty, and already the clubhouse was beginning to grow dark. She crossed to the far wall and snapped on the dozen naked bulbs which lit the warehouse.

'We gonna sit around here 'till then?' asked Adolph impatiently.

'Please yourself,' said Mama. 'You got any better ideas just say.'

'Need a new front tyre for the hog,' Adolph announced. 'Thought I'd shoot round to Bernie's...you wanna come?'

'No thanks,' Elaine snapped quickly. She had long since paid off her debt to Bernie, and didn't particularly want to remind herself of the price she had paid.

Adolph clambered to his feet uncertainly, sensing the tiny wave of antagonism.

'Coming?' he muttered to Freaky.

'Yeah - why not,' said Freaky and rose to join him. They glanced uneasily at Mama before leaving, as though seeking her approval to move.

She glared back at them without expression, feeling once again the little thrill of power deep inside. In the last few weeks, she had become convinced of her total hold over the Angels - she was constantly reminded that their whole lives centred around her orders and her permission. The feeling warmed her.

Finding no direct refusal, Adolph and Freaky left the clubhouse. Long after the roar of their hogs had faded into the distance, Elaine rose slowly to her feet and strolled towards the door. Locking it firmly behind her, she walked to where the

Harley was concealed behind a pile of old tea chests and kicked it into life. The sensuous throb of the engine between her thighs only served to inflame the dull ache which had started in her loins. It was a feeling she had come to know increasingly over the last few months - and one for which there was only one cure.

She drove home to her bedsitter, parked the hog and let herself in. As soon as the door was closed behind her, she started to tug impatiently at the zipper of her costume.

Stepping out of the snake-like skin, she quickly shrugged off her flimsy underclothes and stood naked in front of her full-length mirror.

She stared with undisguised admiration at the reflection of her own body in all its glory. Her hands strayed upwards to cup the full ripeness of her lovely breasts. She toyed with them lovingly, stroking her fingers over the cherry-pink protuberances of her nipples.

Her lips parted slowly, and the ache deep in her belly began to surge up through her body until it was like a liquid fire running through every vein.

She turned to confront her lover, proud to expose her beauty to his blank gaze.

There, pinned on the wall, was her secret lover.

Chopper Harris, dead these long months, smiled down at her.

His picture had been blown up to poster size - and it had the place of honour.

Fuzzy, slightly out of focus and riddled with grey, grainy patches as a result of the enlargement...but nevertheless the well-remembered face of Chopper.

Still staring lovingly at the picture, Elaine sank backwards on to her bed and her hands strayed to explore the hunger of her own body.

The picture watched impassively as she worked herself up to a gradual frenzy, climaxed with a tiny cry of satisfaction, then weakly flopped back to sleep.

She had sworn herself to celibacy when she made her great decision. Apart from her unfortunate, but necessary encounter with Bernie, there had been no other man near her.

Elaine was determined that no Angel should know her, and aware of her own sexuality to realise that a moment of weakness could drag her down.

Sexless, she was Queen of the Angels - an undisputed leader. Just one indiscretion, and she could be dragged down to the level of an ordinary woman...another one of the mindless bitches who opened their legs like coin-operated sex machines.

...But the animal lust was still here under the aloof exterior. It came upon her with ever-increasing frequency, and it made her body scream out for release.

The picture hanging upon her wall was Elaine's one little secret.

CHAPTER SEVEN

ANGEL WEDDING

The clubhouse was alive with pulsing beat music, and an infectious air of total abandon hung in the smoke-filled air.

Mama smiled graciously as she entered, giving the now peremptory clenched-fist salute. She looked around quickly, making a mental note of all important faces.

The guests of honour had not arrived yet - which was just as well. It would give everyone else a good chance to get boozed up so they could give their best. Mama took a can of beer which was thrust towards her and ripped off the ring opener.

She drank greedily, swallowing the contents and flinging the emptied can towards the back of the room. As soon as it left her hand there was another one offered.

Danny the Deathlover pushed his way through the crowd towards her. He saluted briefly, and grasped her arm gently.

He pulled Mama to a quiet corner.

'We picked up the stuff,' he hissed conspiratorially in her ear. 'About a pound and a quarter.'

'How much?' Mama shot back quickly.

'Did in fifty quid...but it's worth four times that at least,' he murmured exuberantly. 'Grass fingered out the guy - he was shit scared the fuzz were on to him.'

To reinforce his words, Danny reached into his originals and pulled out a small flat parcel wrapped up in old newspaper.

Peeling back one corner, he exposed the surface of the chocolate-like block of hashish. Mama nodded appreciatively.

'It was a good pick-up,' she told him. Danny glowed with pleasure and pride.

He hastily bundled the parcel back inside his denim jacket.

'What do you want me to do with it?'

Mama sucked at her teeth reflectively.

'Take off enough stuff for tonight...but get the rest of it out of here,' she said. 'We might attract a bit of fuzz trouble tonight - so we don't want it hanging around.'

Danny winked in acknowledgement.

'I'll see to it, Mama,' he said, and sloped off again, leaving her to do a quick mental calculation on the profit percentage of the deal. Split up into half-ounce lumps, the hash would push out to the kids for at least a couple of hundred.

Trafficking in drugs was just another of the profitable new Angel enterprises.

Mama quickly threw down another two beers in succession, eager to catch on to the elusive spirit of drunken abandon which characterised a good Angel party. She saw Freaky passing by with a half-empty bottle of scotch in his hands, and reached out to snatch it from him. He gave the bottle over willingly and waited patiently while she gulped down a couple of mouthfuls.

'Gonna be a good scene,' he said with a wide grin.

Mama smiled back.

'You bet,' she agreed fervently.

A blast of horns from outside caused heads to whirl towards the door.

A ragged burst of cheers and screams greeted the entry of Superspade looking resplendent in his brand-new denim originals.

He walked slowly across the clubhouse, holding his head up proudly. Tonight was a very special night, and he was deeply aware of the singular honour. The first negro to be initiated into the London Hells Angels - that was really something to be proud of.

Mama rapidly crossed the clubhouse to meet him. He saluted her happily, his big brown face splitting into a toothy grin.

'Hi, Man,' Mama said simply.

'Hi, Mama.'

'You'd better have a drink, Man,' cut in Irish Mick, handing him a can of beer. 'You got plenty in store for you tonight.'

Superspade grinned ruefully. He'd heard plenty, but what was truth and what just part of the myth, he wasn't really sure.

Irish Mick reached out to grasp the denim of his jacket between finger and thumb. He rubbed at it experimentally, feeling the stiffness and resilience of the new cloth.

'We'll soon have these baptised,' he vowed, and turned to throw a knowing wink at Max the Knife, who stood nearby.

It was the signal for Pretty Boy Parritt and Grass to step forward. Max joined them, pulling a wicked-looking sheath knife from his belt as he approached.

Everyone else stood back almost reverently as Max, Pretty Boy and Grass stood in front of the expectant Superspade. Each in turn slowly extended their arm, holding the palm upwards.

'These three guys gave you your participation test,' explained Elaine. 'So they also have the right to blood you first.'

Max fingered the keen edge of the knife reflectively, his cold grey eyes staring unhesitatingly into Superspade's.

He stood unflinching, hypnotised by the hard, strained look on the faces of the three Angels who faced him and by the light flashing on the silver blade.

Slowly, menacingly, Max drew back the knife - holding it in a stabbing position.

Superspade glanced down fearfully at the wicked point of the knife. It was lined up with the middle of his stomach.

The faintest trace of fear had begun to show in his dark eyes. He shifted his feet uncertainly.

Max smiled grimly, and slowly pulled back the knife. He turned to Pretty Boy Parritt and grasped his outstretched hand by the wrist.

Slowly, with all the care of a skilled surgeon, he slipped the point of the knife along Pretty Boy's palm. A tiny trickle of blood bubbled out of the half-inch cut, and collected in a small, dark pool.

Then Grass had his turn, and finally Max turned the knife upon his own hand.

Then, replacing the knife in its sheath, Max smeared his bloody palm over the front of Superspade's spotless denim jacket. The others followed suit, until the front of his originals were well and truly baptised with blood.

The initiation caught tempo now, as other Angels jostled round happily to add their own offerings. Adolph emptied the best part of a can of beer over Superspade's shoulders. Others coughed in their throats, sucking up large gobbets of phlegm which they spat out upon his uniform with gusto.

Elaine stepped forwards. Her face was cold, impassive. The ceremony of initiation was taken seriously by anyone who believed in the Hells Angels.

She mumbled the oath of allegiance quickly. Superspade echoed her words hollowly, anxiously wondering what was next on the agenda. He did not have long to wait.

Two Angels grasped his arms from behind, pulling him down to the floor. Superspade fought off the impulse to resist, realising that he must willingly accept all that they dished out to him.

He lay prone on the floor, looking up at the circle of torturers who stood above him.

With exaggerated calm, Pee Wee and Ethel unzipped their jeans and began the next step in the baptism of his originals. Two hot streams of urine played over his chest and thighs, soaking into the denim and creating small clouds of steam.

To finish, Danny the Deathlover came over, stuck two fingers down the back of his throat and managed to induce a brief spasm of vomiting. The fountain of beer and half-digested food splattered over what had been a new denim jacket.

A chorus of cheers rang round the clubhouse at Danny's supreme effort.

Superspade lay there in his little pool of filth and started to grin happily. That, it appeared, was it. The initiation was complete. He looked over his stained clothing fondly, knowing that these denim clothes were forever after his only official Angel uniform. He must never wash them or wear others on runs or any official turnouts. It was rumoured that a really good set of originals ought to be able to stand up by themselves. Superspade had no doubt that his would pass such a test before many more months passed.

Elaine reached down and helped him to his feet.

'Welcome to the Hells Angels,' she said simply, and a grin at last burst across her face. 'You need a drink,' she added, handing him a four-pint can of bitter. 'Now all you gotta do is empty that can without putting it down,' she snapped. Superspade took a deep breath, raised the can to his lips and started to swallow the beer in huge gulps.

Quite a lot of it bypassed his throat and ran down his chin to join the other staining substances.

With a final, gargantuan effort, he emptied the half-gallon and gave vent to a glorious, reverberating belch which travelled round the clubhouse. There was another chorus of cheers.

Breathless, he stared directly at Elaine.

'Is that it?' he asked.

Mama laughed out loud. 'There usually is one more little thing,' she said. 'But in your case, it doesn't really matter.'

Everyone burst into uproarious laughter. It was usual to take down an initiate's jeans and bestow a generous dollop of black motorcycle grease upon his balls...but as Mama had pointed out, there was no real point in Superspade's case.

Not knowing the joke, Superspade could only look on and smile good-naturedly as everyone collapsed with laughter.

Suddenly it was party time, and every man for himself. The generous supply of beer started to dwindle very quickly as the Angels drank recklessly. Getting well and truly stoned was the next great objective of the evening. Frivolity didn't really begin until there was a nice, overwhelming spirit of drunkenness about.

Huddled in corners, small groups sat cross-legged in circles and passed round joints with great ceremony. The thick, pungent smell of burning hash quickly filled the room to add its own heady vapour to the assorted smells.

The more impatient Angels grabbed birds and asserted their rights for the evening. Mama watched and smiled. There were more than enough girls to go round. Ever since things had started really getting together, the gang had attracted thrill-seeking young dollies like flies to a jampot. Mama appraised some of them, and her beautiful mouth curled into a sadistic sneer. Her eyes roved around until they settled on one particular girl. She was quite new, and judging from the glazed, amazed look on her face, seeing the Hells Angels at a party for the first time.

Mama summoned Danny to her side and pointed over towards the girl.

'Who is she?' she wanted to know.

Danny shrugged.

'Christ knows,' he said. '...I think Fish brought her.'

'Go get him,' snapped Mama. 'And bring the kid over here too.'

Danny loped away in search of Fish - so named because of his bulging eyes, the result of a thyroid deficiency in early childhood.

The girl stared warily across the room at Elaine as Danny nudged her shoulder and pointed. She scrambled to her feet cautiously and headed across the clubhouse.

As she approached Mama, Fish came hurrying across with a worried frown on his face.

'What's up, Mama?' he asked, before Elaine had a chance to

speak to the bewildered girl.

Mama stared at him coldly.

'Did you bring this chick here?' she asked, flicking an icy glance towards the girl.

'Yeah - I brought her along...so what's wrong?'

Fish was on his guard at once, openly aggressive.

'So she's a kid, that's what,' snapped Mama angrily. 'She's too young.' She turned her attention to the trembling girl.

'How old are you, kid?'

The girl lowered her false eyelashes and spoke in a whisper.

'Sixteen,' she muttered.

'Yeah?' sneered Mama, unconvinced. When was your birthday?'

The kid blushed.

'Last week.'

Mama turned to Fish angrily.

'Get her the hell out of here,' she snapped, in a tired, bored voice. 'What do you think we're running... a tea party. This kid's jail-bait.'

Fish shuffled his feet awkwardly, an apologetic expression on his face.

'I thought she was older,' he confessed. '...But she's a really willing kid, Mama - honest!'

Mama looked at him piercingly for a second, then switched back to stare at the girl again. She raised one eyebrow a fraction, showing the light of devilment dancing in her eyes. Mama was smiling, but it was a harsh, cynical smile.

'Yeah?' she questioned again. 'How willing?'

It was a loaded question - and Fish was smart enough to understand the meaning behind it.

'I told you...she's a real game kid,' he repeated stubbornly, trying to stick up for the girl. 'She's all right, Mama, honest.'

The girl herself had recovered some of her composure now, and her natural feminine arrogance began to rise to the surface. Somehow she felt debased, insulted to have a big, tough man like Fish grovelling and apologising for her in front of just another girl.

...And to her, that was all Mama represented.

'I'm quite capable of talking for myself,' she said cuttingly. Her words were directed at Fish, but served also as an indirect challenge to Elaine.

She tossed her pretty blonde head in a defiant gesture, puffing out her chest so that her nymph-like, sensual figure was displayed to its best advantage.

'There ain't nothing I can't do as well as any woman,' she stated proudly. '...Maybe a lot better than some.'

The emphasis on her last words was heavy and obvious...made even more so by the way her eyes blazed defiantly into Elaine's.

The look on Mama's face hardened into an icy mask of undiluted hate. She wasn't going to take any insulting inferences against her sexuality from a sixteen-year-old scrubber.

Elaine stared at her silently and thoughtfully for a moment.

'I'm gonna give you a chance to prove that statement, kid,' she muttered finally. 'You're gonna pull a train for the cabaret spot.'

The kid's eyes flickered nervously for a moment. Although she hadn't heard the expression before, she had a fairly good idea what it meant, and for a second she regretted putting herself in such an awkward situation. She remained silent, forcing herself to remain outwardly calm.

It was Fish who voiced all the objections.

'You can't do that, Mama,' he blurted out angrily. 'This is the kid's first trip. You can't just sling her in at the deep end.'

Elaine's eyes narrowed to slits.

'Who says I can't?' she challenged.

'I just ain't gonna let you,' shouted back Fish defiantly.

Mama's eyes were blazing now. Her bottom lip twitched almost imperceptibly - but even the most casual onlooker would have seen that she was rattled.

This was a direct challenge to her authority - and Elaine didn't like it one bit. The mood was ugly.

She spoke slowly, as if summoning great patience and self-control. Her voice was flat and unemotional, but blistering with hidden menace.

'Fish,' she murmured quietly. 'You ought to have learned by now that I give the orders around here.'

Fish ought to have sensed the venom in her voice and played it smart.

He didn't. His anger had bubbled too far past the boiling point to cool down now.

'Well then it's about time we started to stand on our own two feet,' he responded blisteringly. 'I ain't the only one around here who's pissed off with taking orders from a goddamned woman.'

He glanced quickly around the clubhouse, noting how a crowd was rapidly building up around them. Danny the Deathlover looked at Fish warningly - but it was too late.

The gauntlet had been thrown down. The dice had been cast.

Mama didn't waste time with any more words. Blind with rage, she stepped forward and with one, quick movement, brought her knee up under Fish's groin.

He doubled up with a scream of agony, and sank to the ground with his hands cupped around his testicles. Mama's booted foot drew back in a swinging arc, and slammed back against the side of his head like a power-assisted pendulum.

Fish didn't make a sound. He was out cold.

Mama bent over him slowly and dug her long nails into the edge of the Angel badge sewn on to the back of his originals. With one tug, she ripped off his colours and threw them across the room contemptuously.

The girl stared down at the unconscious body of Fish for a few seconds. She was struck speechless...but not for long.

Suddenly she erupted into a screaming, spitting ball of female fury. She launched herself at Elaine, fingers reaching out to pull at her long blonde hair.

'You bitch,' she screamed insanely, as her fingers made contact and curled into the thick tresses.

Elaine's arm shot up in defence. Her long fingernails raked across the girl's unprotected face, leaving claw-marks like those of a wildcat. As the kid screamed with pain, Mama drew back one fist and delivered a punishing blow to the girl's belly.

Her grip on Elaine's hair fell free as all the wind gushed out of her body. Casually, with sadistic precision, Mama grasped the kid round the throat in her left hand and rose her right hand to the level of the girl's face.

She slapped her across the cheek with the flat of her palm, then returned across the other cheek with the back of her hand. Again and again her hand slapped back and forth across the kid's pretty face, until it was flushed scarlet with bruises and blood. Tiny cuts opened up where Mama's heavy dress rings had torn out small pieces of skin.

Mama continued slapping the girl until her arm was tired. Then, with a contemptuous sneer, she placed one hand full in the girl's chest and pushed her away.

The kid staggered backwards, tripped over the prone figure of Fish and collapsed in an untidy heap on top of him.

Mama glanced at Danny sneeringly.

'Get 'em out of here,' she snapped, and turned away.

The clubhouse was deathly quiet. No one moved, no one spoke. Silently, the assembled Angels stood and stared down at the two bodies in awe.

Superspade snaked across the floor, bent down and picked up the colours which Mama had ripped from Fish's denims.

'Hell - it takes a bloody long time to get into this outfit...but you can sure as Hell get out in a hurry,' he shouted, waving them high in the air.

The tension broke. A nervous ripple of laughter broke out, slowly gathering momentum until it exploded into a wave of mirth.

Danny and Max the Knife bent down to scoop up Fish and the girl. They dragged them across the stone floor to the door, and bundled them unceremoniously into the street outside.

'...And don't get any funny ideas about revenge,' Danny spat at the groaning Fish. 'We're 100 per cent behind Mama...and don't you forget it.' He closed the door with a bang.

Mama slapped her hands together as if to brush off the dust.

'Right then...let's get back to the party,' she called out in an amused voice.

With whoops of pleasure, the Angels set about consuming the remaining booze with gusto.

Someone slipped a heavy rock number on to the stereo unit and the clubhouse once more trembled with the pounding music.

The hectic events of the last few minutes evaporated as quickly as they had begun.

Danny the Deathlover grabbed two cans of beer, opened them both and carried one over to Mama.

'You was great,' he said, with a proud smile on his face.

Elaine accepted his admiration graciously.

'Thank you Danny,' she murmured with mock sweetness and

a demure little smile. She glanced momentarily at her watch.

'Juice ought to be here soon,' she pointed out. 'It's quarter to ten.'

Danny nodded absently.

'Maybe he changed his mind,' he said with a grin. 'Or he's gotten absolutely stoned out of his mind somewhere.'

A flying beer bottle whizzed past Danny's head as he spoke. It splintered into fragments against the wall. Danny glanced round casually towards the booze supply, where half a dozen Angels rummaged frantically among the pile of empty crates and discarded cans.

'Looks like supplies are running low,' he said pointedly.

Elaine turned and pursed her lips reflectively.

'Yeah. Looks like you're right. I guess you'd better take a tenner out of funds, grab a couple of fellers and go get some more beer.'

'No need,' said Danny, smiling. He gestured towards the clubhouse door with his thumb.

A mountain of beer crates was slowly staggering into the clubhouse. Behind the precariously-balanced pile came 'Juice' James, half a dozen of his immediate follows...and, of course, his bride-to-be.

Julie, Juice's favourite mama, was being carried, chair-lift style, by four burly Angels. Sitting up there in her human sedan chair, she looked as though she was floating on her own little private cloud. She probably was...a private cloud concocted out of drugs, alcohol and her wild spirit which had endeared her to Juice over the last two months.

She had been one of the sheep until Juice had bestowed his regular favours upon her. Rumour had it that she had once pulled a train for seventeen Angels in a row...but no one could actually swear to being present at the time. At least fifty Angels, however, claimed to know someone who was, or swore to have completely authentic knowledge of the event through some mysterious third party.

Now Juice was elevating Julie to the exalted rank of his 'old lady'. He was establishing sole rights through an official Angel marriage ceremony. After that, she would be his exclusive private property...second only in value to his hog.

The party's entrance was greeted warmly. Half the people present made a spectacular scramble for the fresh booze supply as soon as it touched the floor.

It was left to Mama to actually speak to Juice and his girl.

She crossed the room, extending her arm in the clenched-fist salute.

'Good to see you, Man.'

Juice peered at her through slit eyes and a mist of intoxication.

Recognition slowly dawned on him and his face split into a drunken leer.

'Hiya, Mama...I brought some beer.'

'So I noticed,' Elaine replied with a smile. 'Just in time, as it happens.'

The four Angels carrying Julie deposited her on the floor with a hard bump. She didn't seem to notice it. She sat happily in a small pool of spilled beer and stared, glassy-eyed into space.

'Stoned?' asked Mama.

'Stoned,' confirmed Juice.

Elaine looked at the drugged figure of Julie with a faint trace of pity. It was obvious that Juice was turning her on to his own mainline habit. Juice was a speed-freak...hopelessly addicted to injecting himself with intravenous amphetamines. It was from this habit that he got his Angel name of 'Juice'.

Elaine knew enough about drugs to know that amphetamine addiction was potentially more destructive than heroin. It literally ate away the brain cells, until the brain resembled a crumbling Swiss cheese. Luckily for most, death came long before that point was reached.

Juice followed Mama's gaze and shrugged apologetically. 'She wanted to try,' he said weakly.

'Why don't you tell her to stick to pills?' said Elaine, then turned away and dropped the subject. It was none of her business.

'She'll be OK in a while,' Juice reassured her. 'Meanwhile, we ought to get things ready...eh?'

Mama nodded. 'Get your boys to bring your hog inside,' she muttered.

Juice gestured to a couple of his boys, who were avidly consuming their share of the beer. They finished their bottles and staggered outside once again.

They wheeled in the shining, resplendent hog with almost funereal ceremony. It stood in the centre of the room, propped up on its footrest.

The hog would serve as the 'altar' for the irreligious ceremony which was to follow.

Juice strolled over to Julie and yanked her roughly to her feet. He slapped her across the face a couple of times and the girl's glazed eyes seemed to clear slightly.

'What's on, Man?' she asked in a weak, distant voice.

'Don't worry about it, babe,' mumbled Juice. 'Just stay on your feet...OK?'

Julie grinned stupidly, and burst into a fit of giggling. Juice slapped her again - hard.

The giggles subsided at once.

'OK...I think we're ready,' Juice called across to Mama. 'Let's get on with it.'

His small band of followers clustered around the 'altar' as Juice half-dragged Julie across the room to the hog. He stood her on one side of the bike and instructed two buddies to hold her up. Then he went to the other side of the hog and stood facing her over the polished black saddle.

Still maintaining the air of ceremony, his lieutenant placed the 'bible' gently on the saddle with reverent gestures.

The 'bible' was a motorcycle manual - yet another link between the Hells Angel and his two-wheeled deity.

Juice reached forward and placed the palm of his hand upon the manual. With a little help and guidance, Julie's hand was pressed down next to it.

The words which Mama intoned were a hotch-potch of phrases and snippets from church wedding ceremonies, registry offices and ideas picked up from television programmes. The words didn't really matter, nobody worried unduly. The ceremony was all-important.

The travesty of religious incantation lasted only a few seconds. Words and phrases such as 'do you take...', 'For better and for worse...' and 'to have and to hold' tumbled out and fell meaninglessly upon the air.

It was time for the exchanging of rings.

Juice's lieutenant delved into the pocket of his jacket and produced the 'sacred' jewellery.

Two brass washers - originally part of a Triumph Thunderbird - had been painstakingly filed down, reamed out and polished until they shone brightly.

The two rings were rubbed for effect one more time against denim and deposited upon the leather saddle.

Juice picked one up, lifted Julie's limp hand and slipped it carefully on to her finger.

The second part was more difficult. Julie's fingers shook and trembled as she tried to grasp the small washer. Eventually, with dextrous manipulation from her helpers, she managed to jam the ring over Juice's finger.

Mama slammed the bible shut and stepped back from the happy couple.

'Time to do your thing, Man,' she whispered softly.

A lecherous leer crept across Juice's face. Stepping round the hog, he bent to scoop Julie up in his arms. He carried her across the clubhouse.

The crowd of Angels stepped back dutifully to let him pass, clearing a small area around one of the dirty mattresses thrown down on the floor.

Juice stood over it, dumped Julie down and began to fumble with the zipper of his jeans.

To the accompaniment of whistles, cheers and cat-calls, he sank down on top of her.

In an Angel wedding ceremony, the practice of simply kissing the bride was considered too tame.

Juice consummated his 'marriage' hastily and inexpertly. The clinical operation only lasted a few seconds. Finished, he stood up, adjusted his clothing and glanced down dispassionately at Julie.

She had lapsed into unconsciousness.

Juice grinned, shrugged his shoulders and turned away from her. Slapping his arms around the shoulders of his two nearest Angel compatriots, he steered them towards the beer supply.

'Jeezus,' he swore. 'Screwing makes me bloody thirsty.'

The three of them staggered towards the booze without another glance at the girl on the floor.

Someone helpfully emptied half a can of beer over her face,

but it didn't seem to help.

Everyone promptly forgot about her and the party resumed with renewed gusto. An individual didn't seem to matter...only the group identity of the Hells Angels was of any real importance.

The floor was littered with broken bottles and drunken bodies. Pools of vomit filled the corners, where Angels went politely to flash up any excess drink to make room for the next beer.

Inspired by the example of Juice James, two or three couples had gained possession of the precious mattresses and were endeavouring to make love under a constant barrage of flying feet and hurled debris. Over by the record player, Irish Mick and Slim were playing flying saucers with old records. The thin black discs whizzed through the air above the heads of the milling crowd. Someone caught a glancing blow in the eyes, screamed with pain and charged across the room to pour a can of beer over Slim's head. The game ceased abruptly.

The remaining hours of Saturday ticked away relentlessly. Some of the female guests led their Angel escorts outside with blunt promises of rewards to come after the necessary lift home. Small groups from other chapters gradually banded together, decided to hit the road and sauntered outside to their hogs.

The last empty beer can clattered to the floor and a comparative quietness fell upon those remaining.

It was three-thirty in the morning.

The party was over.

Mama looked around the floor, littered with the bodies of sleeping or unconscious Angels. She sought out Danny the Deathlover, ensconced on one of the mattresses with a girl called Sparky.

'About time I quit,' she muttered to him. Danny looked up bleary-eyed, grinned drunkenly and giggled.

'Want me to lock up?' he asked.

'You gonna be around for long?' Elaine asked him.

'Reckon I'm here for the night,' said Danny, and patted Sparky affectionately upon the rump. 'You can lock up as you leave...I'll let anybody out who wants to blow.'

'OK.' Mama grinned proudly. 'Some party - huh?'

'You bet,' agreed Danny fervently.

Elaine walked slowly across the quietened clubhouse to the door. She looked briefly back, flipped out the light switch and closed the door behind her.

Outside, the November air was bitterly cold. As Elaine kicked the Harley into life and cruised slowly along the darkened canal alleyways, the wind knifed through her leathers and a thick sweater to chill her to the bones.

The cold seemed to drive out the fuzzy cobwebs which had been filling her head back in the clubhouse. The alcohol seeping through her bloodstream was purified, somehow rarefied, so that the heady sense of intoxication remained without any of the slurring effects upon her consciousness.

Suddenly, Elaine felt wide awake once again and her mind was honed to knife-sharp precision. She no longer wanted to return home to her lonely, boring little room.

Thinking of the nearest warm place to go, she turned into Liverpool Road and blasted up it until she came to the Angel, Islington. Ignoring a red traffic light, she streaked across the junction and headed for company. There, a long line of parked lorries announced her destination.

She parked the hog, dismounted and strolled into the small all-night transport cafe.

It was warm and cosy. The small, smoke-filled cafe was crowded with long-distance lorry drivers who were taking a brief respite for a hot cup of tea and a pie before setting off again on the long haul up country to the North.

Heads turned in her direction as she pushed open the door, and several wolf-whistles followed her across to the serving hatch.

She propped herself up against it and stared back at the suspicious, accusing eyes with a chilling expression. The buzz of conversation usually present in the cafe had dropped to a whisper at her entrance. Lorry drivers were an insular lot - they resented and distrusted the presence of outsiders.

Elaine ordered a coffee and carried it across to the only empty table. She sat down, and absently stirred in three teaspoonfuls of sugar.

Gradually, the wary eyes flickered away from her, and the cafe returned to normal. Conversations started up again, and the drivers once again buried themselves in friendly communication with their own kind.

The talk was mostly of a professional nature, as drivers and their mates discussed engine troubles, roadworks and crafty new ways of avoiding well-known bottlenecks.

Occasionally, someone would crack a filthy joke, and a ripple of raucous laughter would run round the cafe. Someone started to recount a supposedly true tale about a nymphomaniac hitch-hiker he had picked up, and the conversation ended in a jeer of disbelief.

Elaine toyed with her cup and listened with vague interest. Behind her, someone started talking in subdued tones of a robbery. Elaine pricked up her ears. This conversation seemed to be much more interesting.

It was a young lorry driver, recounting the story of a recent hijacking. He described how thieves had stolen his mate's lorry from outside a transport cafe in the Midlands. He lowered his voice to a whisper when he described the load and its value, but Elaine was just able to hear.

Fifty thousand quid's worth of cigarettes! It was quite a haul. Elaine's eyebrows raised slightly in awe.

She drank her coffee hastily and stood up.

As she climbed on to the Harley, the thought of a fifty-thousand pound hijacking was rolling in her mind like a half-finished film script. She could see it all in visual mental images...robbery on the open road...the fast, screaming getaway...the crates of precious loot being unloaded.

Elaine could well imagine herself as the Queen of big-time crime - leader of the gang who struck terror into the hearts and minds of the citizens.

She pictured the long-distance lorries, rolling through the night along the motorways like modern-day stagecoaches. The thought of the black band of Hells Angels, riding into the glory and excitement of a life of highway robbery. It was the day of the highwaymen brought up to date; a romantic image of the heroic criminal who had been a popular myth since Robin Hood.

She could be a British Bonny Parker.

The only thing missing would be the figure of a Clyde Barrow to ride beside her.

Gradually, her thoughts returned to reality, and the daydream

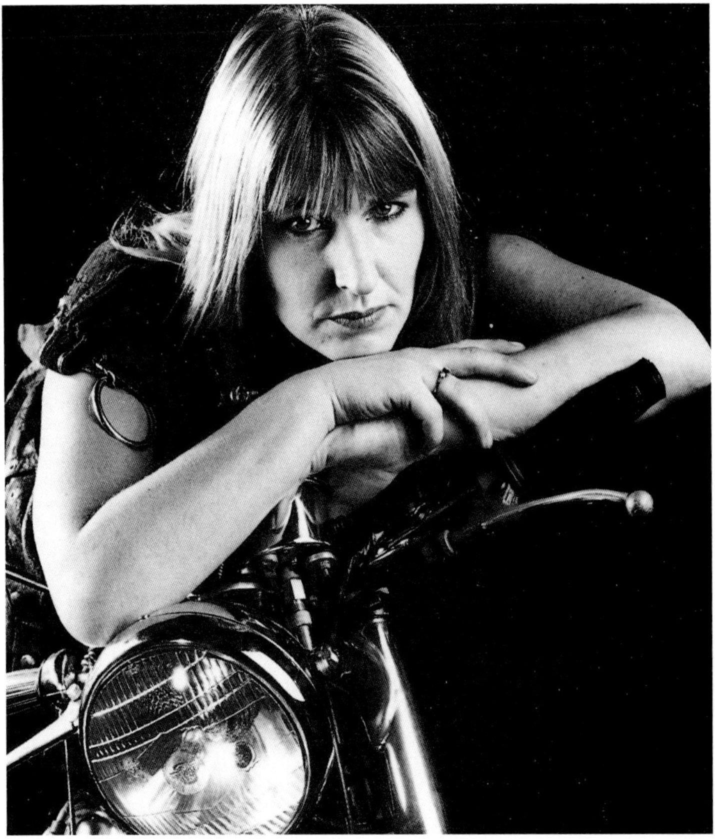

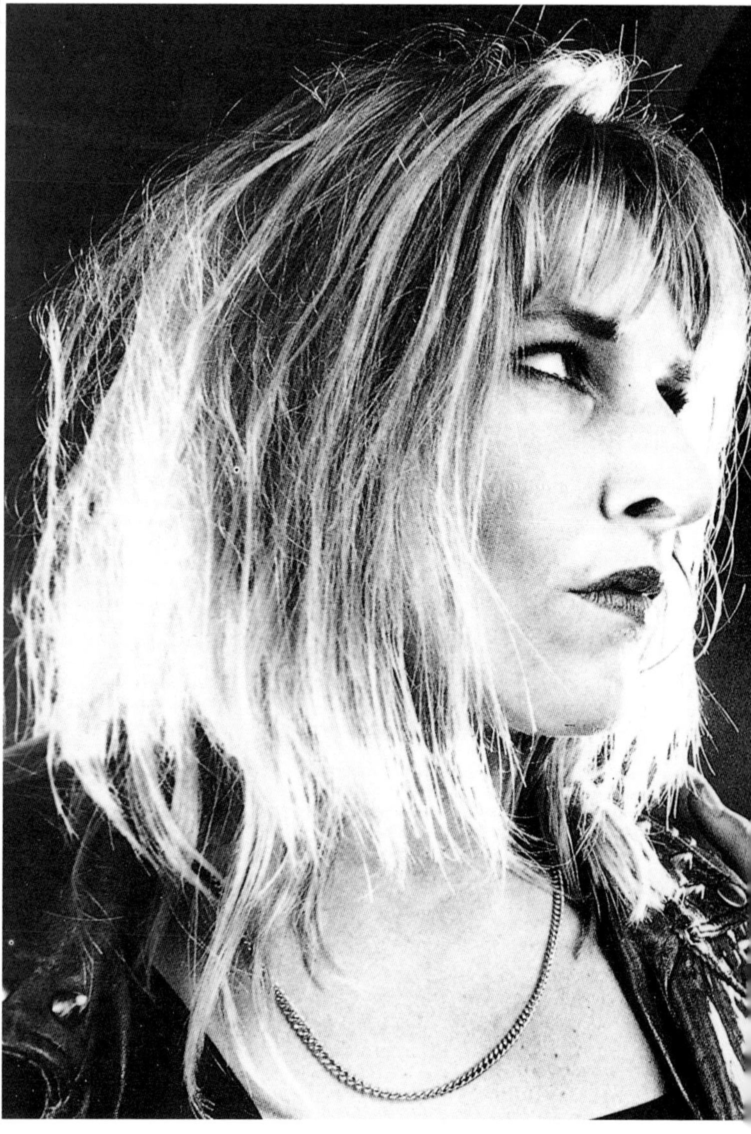

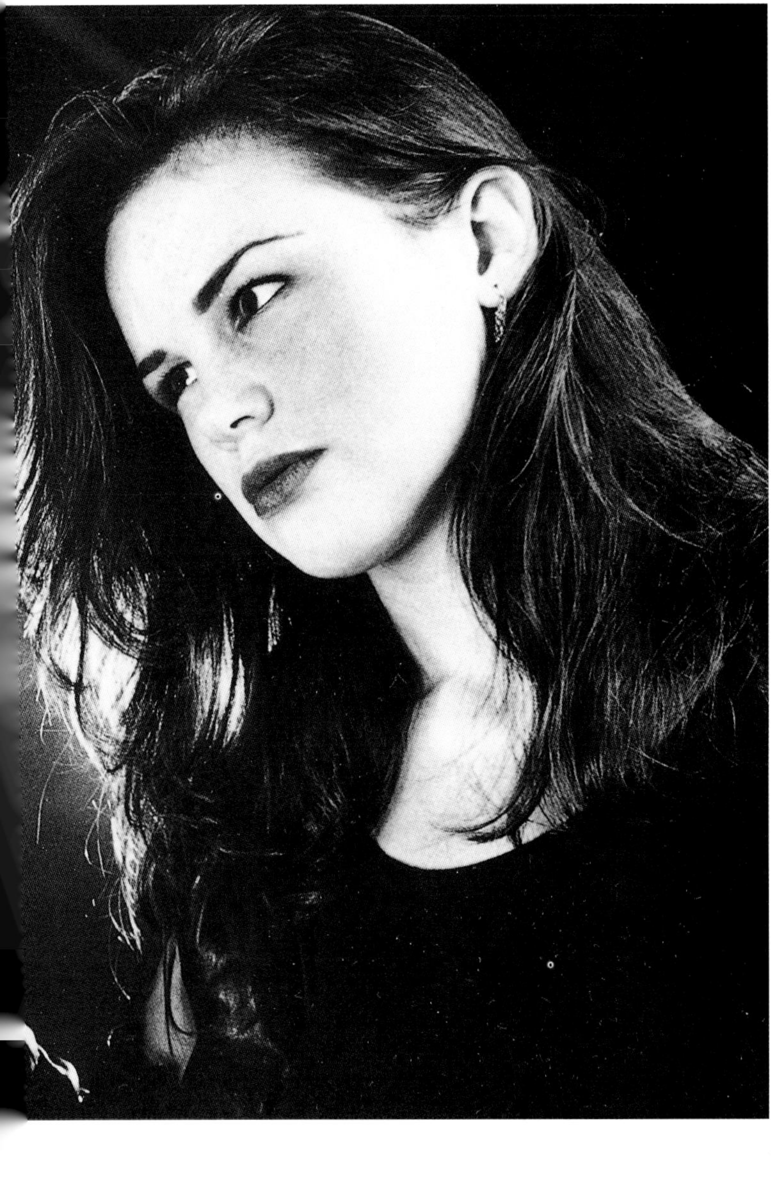

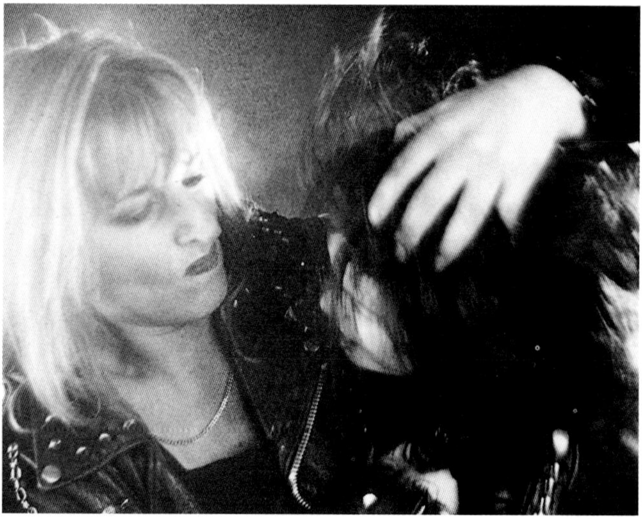

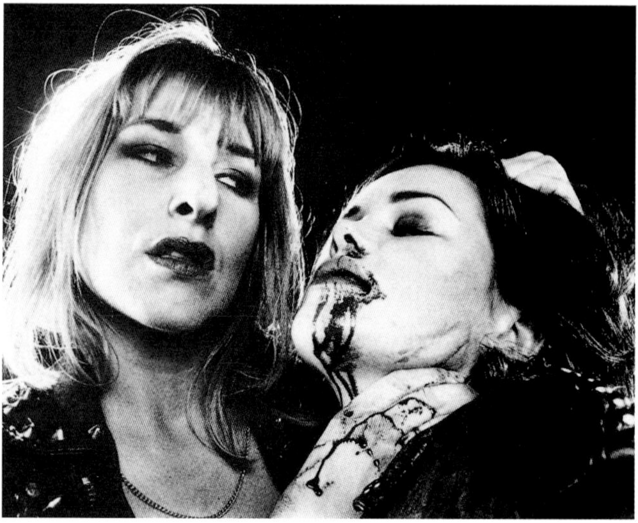

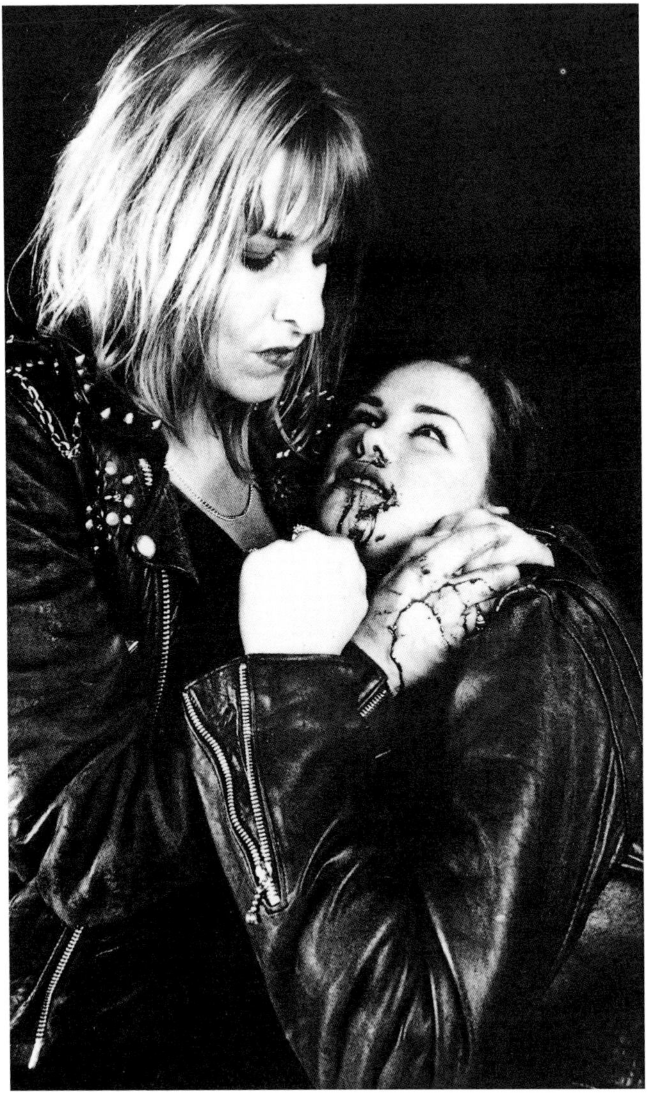

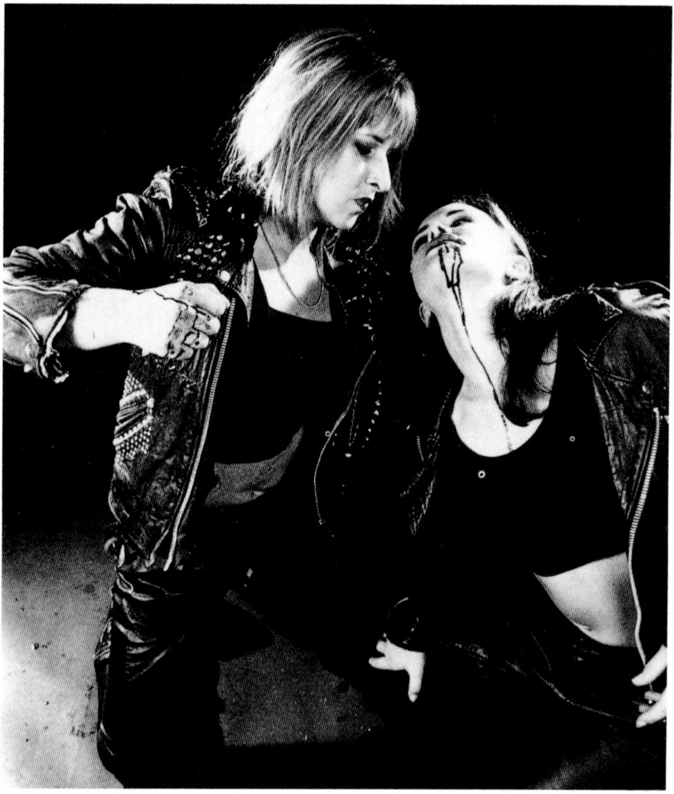

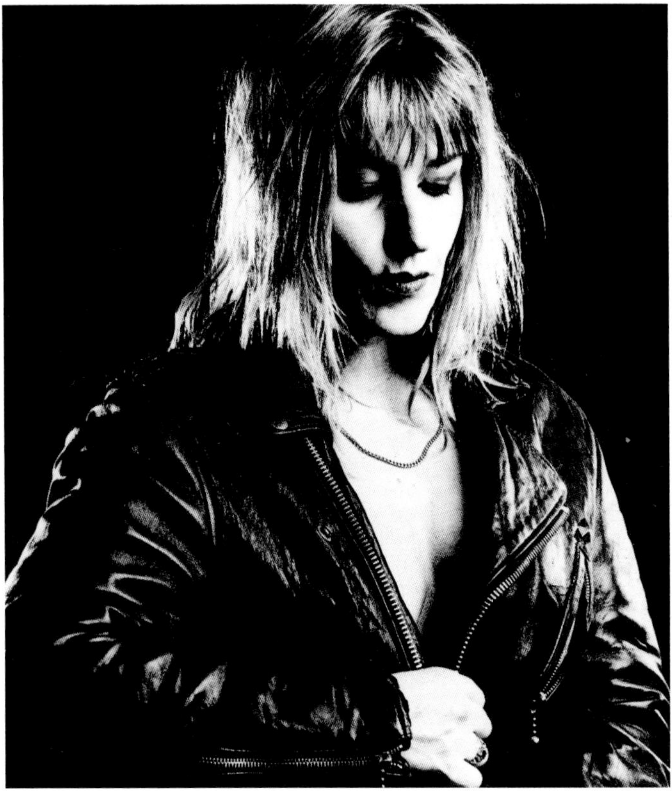

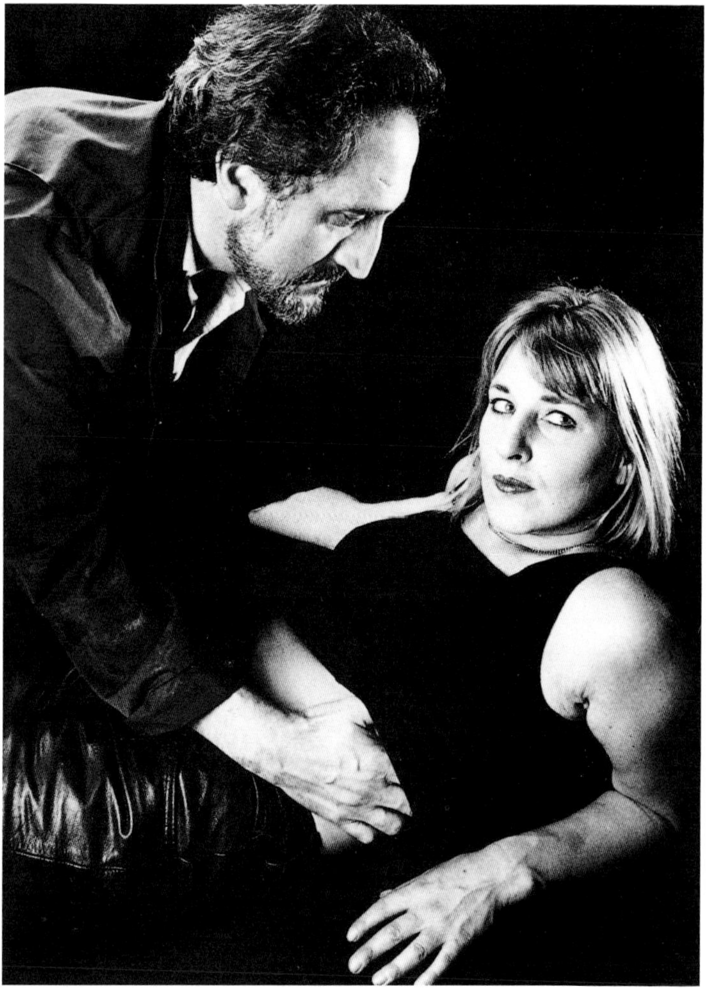

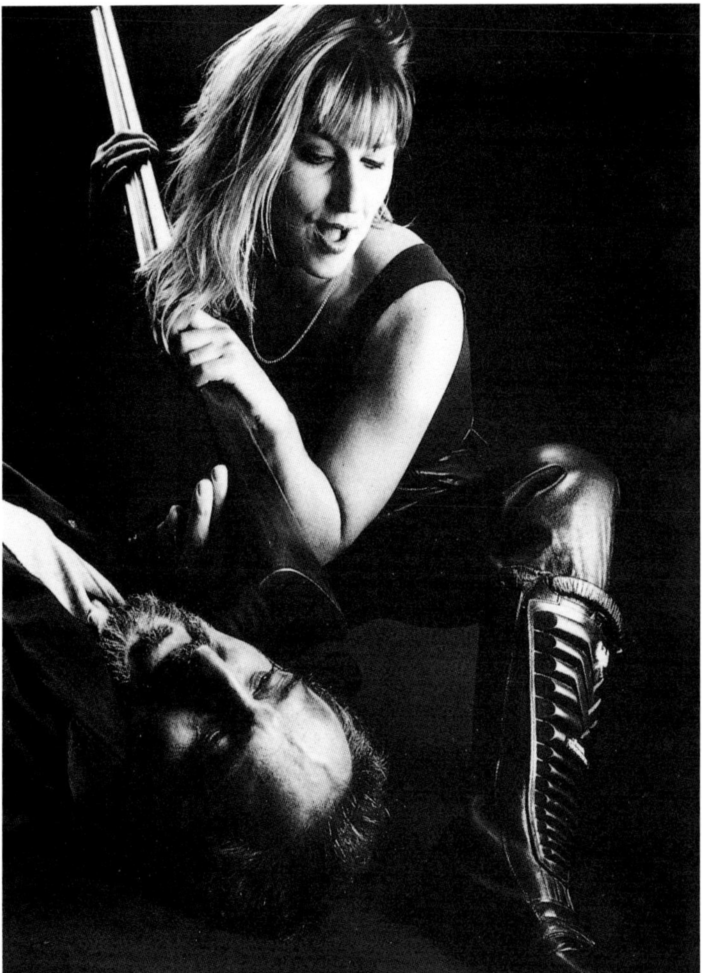

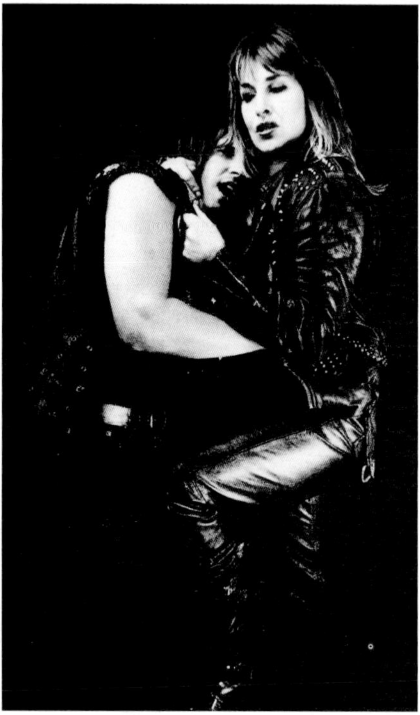
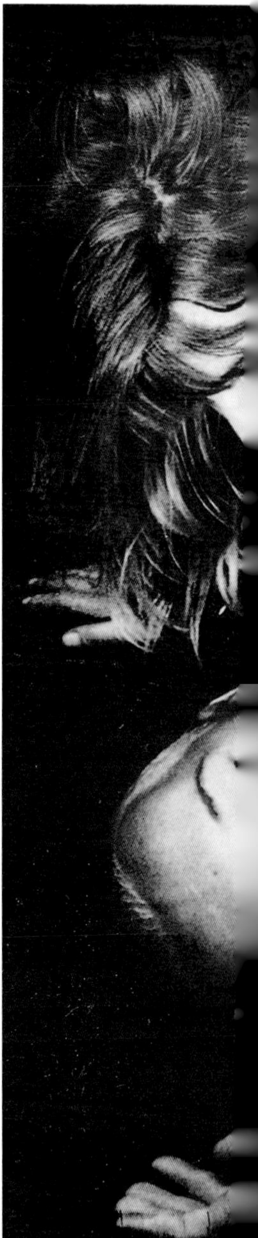

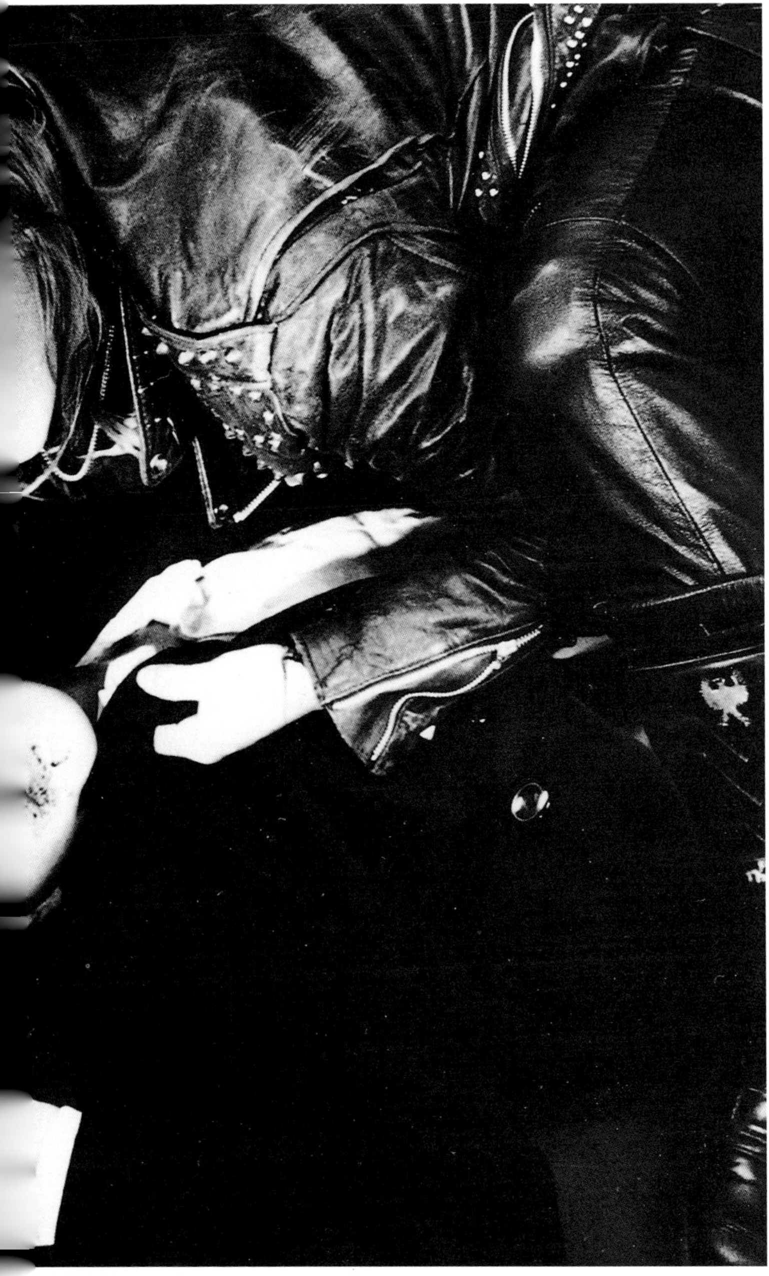

Concept / Art Direction — Nigel Wingrove
Photography — Chris Bell
Hair and Make up — Ashley Mae
Models: — Mama — Heather
Biker Girl — Linsey   **Biker** — Paul   **Man** — Georgio
All pictures posed by models — ie don't try this at home

faded. All that, perhaps, some time in the future. Right now, there were more immediate things to think about.

The incident with Fish earlier in the evening had rattled her more than she dared show. It was not that she had been shown up by it...on the contrary. Big Mama had come out of the encounter fairly well. What really mattered was the fact that he had been able to question her. It meant that her supremacy was not unchallenged...that her hold over the Angels was only a tenuous one.

Seeing herself through other eyes, Elaine realised with something of a jolt that her image was incomplete - lacking in some indefinable quality which could seal her authority. She had trust, she had respect, and all the other necessary trappings of a leader.

What, then, was missing?

A seething anger overwhelmed her suddenly as she cursed her own sexuality. Somehow, she felt that the root of the problem lay there, in the fact that she was a woman. Yet the Angels had been more willing to follow her than she had ever dreamed. It had all been just a little too easy.

Perhaps that was what was so wrong. There should have been a fight, a struggle. No leader could ever win the complete and utter admiration of followers without some obvious sign of bravery or superiority in battle.

...Only there had been no battle to fight and win. No chance to be brave, show class...no adversity to overcome.

A sad thought crept into her mind...almost painful in its sudden, blinding revelation of the true nature of things. In this unusual insight into the situation, Elaine could see the Hells Angels as what they truly were underneath the created myths and forced creeds.

They were merely a pathetic band of failures - dropouts from a civilisation they couldn't cope with. Because they were unable to belong, they cowered together in fear and trusted only their own massed numbers.

Of course! Fear was the key. Failure the final answer to the entire puzzle. Individually they were nothing - even less than nothing because they had no real motivation in life. Sheep-like, they followed codes only because it gave them a pattern for existence. They expressed violence because it was the easiest escape valve for fear and uncertainty. They followed her so unquestioningly because they had to have a leader. The identity of that leader didn't really matter.

...And of herself - what? What was Big Mama's little key? Elaine evaded the self-questioning with a violent effort - forcing her mind to escape back into fantasies of power and domination.

Somewhere deep in the recesses of her subconscious mind, two rival factions came together to give battle, fight or control. Between them, a schizophrenic personality looked on and waited. The conscious brain drew down a heavy shutter to protect itself from harsh realities.

Elaine thrust back the throttle savagely and felt a surge of power shudder through the Harley. It leapt forward, the sudden acceleration like an act of aggression against unknown enemies.

Mama headed home, weary again and desperate for the blanketing release of sleep.

Tomorrow, all the doubts and bad thoughts would be effectively removed. Like the alcohol souring in her stomach, the unwanted fears would be expelled in poison waste.

CHAPTER EIGHT

BLOODY CHRISTMAS

Christmas Eve came, but the Star of Bethlehem carefully bypassed certain areas of North London. The spirit of goodwill to all men was not imparted to the Hells Angels.

Ethel slammed his clenched fist against the clubhouse wall and swore viciously.

'Christ! Do you fellers realise it's Christmas? We oughtta get out and really smash the hell out of something tonight.'

Freaky nodded sagely.

'Yeah,' he agreed morosely. 'Ain't gonna be much of a Christmas if we don't get some action.'

'Seems to me,' put in Grass reflectively, '...that we ought to do something really special...Sort of in honour of the occasion, so to speak.'

A chorus of assent rippled round, as the assembled Angels realised that Grass had encapsulated their feelings into his brief speech. Tonight was a very special night - it deserved very special treatment.

Mama sat quietly, content to listen and assess the mood. She too was wondering what action to plan for the evening. She counted heads. There were twenty Angels and seven birds.

'We ain't got much strength,' she pointed out casually. 'Best thing we can do is get out and meet up a few more riders.'

Danny the Deathlover pursed his lips reflectively.

'Where do you reckon?'

Mama thought for a moment.

'Matlock's as good a bet as any,' she concluded at length.

Danny nodded agreeably.

'Yeah. I suppose so,' he mumbled. He scrambled to his feet. 'Well?'

'So what the hell are we waiting for?' asked Mama, rising to join him. 'Let's go get stinking drunk, at least.'

The Angels jumped to their feet eagerly.

'Better leave a note on the door,' Mama said to Danny, 'Just in case anyone else shows up here.'

'Yeah. OK,' said Danny grabbing a felt-tip pen and a sheet of paper from the junk store as he walked towards the door.

He scribbled a brief message - 'Matlock Arms' - and pinned it to the clubhouse door as they left.

The pub was surprisingly empty, considering it was seven-thirty of a Christmas Eve.

Then again, maybe it wasn't surprising at all, considered Mama, since the Angels made up ninety per cent of the pub's clientele these days. Since adopting the place over two months ago, most of the old customers had quickly found other places to do their drinking. It was a lot safer that way.

Pete the publican greeted them with an icy smile as they sauntered in.

'Merry Christmas,' he said without any great warmth.

'Really?' replied Danny the Deathlover cynically. Pete shrugged, and busied himself serving beers.

Mama strolled over to the jukebox, gave it a vicious kick and smiled with satisfaction as the green 'select' light snapped on.

Pete pretended not to notice as she stabbed out a combination on the selector buttons.

What was the point of complaining? One false word from him and there would be a heavy boot through the perspex front of the machine. At least while it remained in working order, some of his customers used the old fashioned method of inserting coins.

'Seen any of the boys tonight?' asked Danny as the publican pulled his pint.

'Nope,' came the quick reply. 'But it's early, ain't it?'

'Yeah,' agreed Danny. 'I guess they'll be along later.'

His eyes strayed to a charity stocking hung on the side of a hot snack cabinet. Inside it, tucked on top of the small coins and fruit-machine tokens, lay a crumpled pound note - obviously thrown in by some well-meaning drunk imbued with the Christmas spirit and a few too many whiskies.

He flipped a 50-pence coin across the counter as payment for his beer. The coin skidded across the smooth Formica surface of the counter, spun over the edge and rolled to the floor. Pete bent to scrabble after it.

Danny's hand moved with the speed of a snake. His fingers deftly reached into the top of the stocking, coiled around the note and pulled it out in one smooth movement. He bundled it into his pocket and casually looked back at the charity appeal.

It was for crippled children.

Danny silenced his momentary qualm of conscience by

reminding himself that there were always other mugs to make up the money.

In any case, he could think of better things to do with a quid than a one-legged kid could.

If Pete noticed the loss when he handed Danny his change, he conveniently forgot to mention it.

The Angels slurped down their drinks greedily and called for another round. They stood around the bar awkwardly, shifting from foot to foot with restlessness. Mama eyed them carefully, only too well aware of the moody, expectant atmosphere. They wanted action, and it was her responsibility to give it to them. She racked her brains for suitable courses of action, but nothing spread readily to mind. While she tried to think, it was best to let them drink, allow the violence to simmer for a while.

The door of the pub swung open and a small group of Angels strolled in to join them. Elaine glanced up at the clock on the wall. It was now almost eight o'clock.

They continued to drink in silence.

A choking roar of hog engines being throttled back outside announced the arrival of another small contingent. Mama's glance flickered to the door as Juice James walked in, followed by Julie and two of his riders.

Juice did not look at all happy. Mama noticed that he walked towards her with a pronounced limp.

'What's up, Man?' she asked him. Juice only glared at her sullenly. It was Julie who answered for him.

'Got done over last night, didn't he,' she muttered. 'Bloody Pakis carved him up.'

'Hurt bad?' Mama asked Juice. He shrugged the question off.

'I'm walking, ain't I?' he shot back without humour.

'Yeah - and you bloody well shouldn't be,' said Julie with vehemence. She turned to Mama. 'Sixteen bleeding stitches he's got in his side - and the crazy bastard still insists on riding.'

Juice whirled on her angrily, and a sudden grunt of pain was torn from his lips at the movement. He clenched his teeth to hide the pain.

'Why won't you quit nagging?' he hissed sharply. 'I keep telling ya I'm all right.'

Mama smiled inwardly. Juice was showing real class...it was

obvious that his injuries were more serious than he was willing to admit.

The smile faded and serious concern crossed her face.

'Tell us about it, Man.' she said slowly. 'What happened?'

'Four Pakis jumped us as we came out of a pub,' he said simply. 'One of the bastards shoved a bloody great blade in me guts.'

'Would you recognise them again?' asked Mama.

The ghost of a grin flickered across Juice's face as he attempted to be funny.

'No,' he said. 'The bastards all look alike to me - I can't tell one jungle-bunny from another.'

'Where was it?' Mama wanted to know.

'Stepney way,' said Juice. 'They got some sort of community centre down there or something.'

'Yeah - I heard about that,' put in Pretty Boy Parritt. 'It was opened a few weeks ago. There's hundreds of the black buggers.'

'Well - we wanted something to do night. Now we got it,' said Mama eagerly. 'We'll teach the bastards they can't get away with mugging an Angel. Reckon we ought to get down to this community centre and show 'em a few things.'

'We're light-handed,' Danny reminded her.

'So we'll have to tool up, won't we?' Mama shot back crushingly. '...Anyway, with the hogs we can strike fast and get the hell out of it before they can hit back.'

She glanced round the pub at the dubious faces. They didn't care for the idea too much. It wasn't Angel practice to go marching in when they knew they would be outnumbered.

'What's the matter with you mothers?' Mama screamed. 'You yellow or something?'

'I certainly ain't that,' called out Superspade with a laugh. Mama looked at him suddenly, having forgotten his presence. She looked at his big black face and felt awkward.

'You don't have to come, Man,' she mumbled understandingly.

Some of the other Angels looked at Superspade with embarrassment. He stared back at them for a moment, questioningly. Then recognition dawned and his face split into one of its huge, white-toothed grins.

'Shit...you don't have to worry about me,' he guffawed. 'I hate them friggin Pakis as much as you do...Hell, Man, they're bloody niggers, ain't they?'

As usual, his good humour was infectious. The Angels relaxed into comfortable laughter.

'Well...what do you say?' asked Mama after a brief pause. 'Danny?'

Danny the Deathlover looked at her calmly, then glanced around at the worried faces behind him.

'Are we gonna let those coons think they can push the Hells Angels around?' he shot at them. The response was far from encouraging.

Danny looked back at Mama and shrugged apologetically.

'I guess we all just need a few more beers to warm us up,' he explained, and called to the publican for service.

Juice James grinned happily at Mama.

'Thanks Mama,' he said simply. 'I hoped you'd give me a chance to get back at those bastards.'

Elaine looked grim.

'You ain't gonna do much participating tonight, Juice,' she told him sternly. 'Not with stitches in your gut you ain't.'

'That's right, Mama. You tell him,' put in Julie sharply.

Juice looked at her scornfully.

'Jeezus...I'd never have married you if I'd known you was gonna be a nagger,' he muttered with a grudging affection. Julie beamed up at him, basking in his reflected light.

'You big slob,' she said lovingly.

Pete leaned across the counter in conspiratorial fashion.

'You kids out for trouble tonight?' he asked casually.

'Never touch the stuff,' Mama shot back at him quickly. 'And you don't want to start, don't ask so many questions.'

The publican shrugged, and moved along the bar to serve another customer. It wasn't up to him to understand these kids.

Time passed. Several drinks later, the assembled Angels were noticeably more aggressive, more optimistic about their chances in Stepney.

'We'll slaughter 'em,' said Grass into a half-empty pint mug. 'Teach 'em to come over here taking over the flamin' country.'

'Yeah...well if we hang around here much longer, they'll all have emigrated to where they came from,' muttered Danny the

Deathlover impatiently. 'Come on, you lazy mothers...drain up and let's get going.'

The Angels threw down the rest of their drinks and started to crowd towards the door.

'Where is this place?' Mama asked Pretty Boy as they hovered around the hogs.

'I'll show you,' promised Pretty. 'Just follow me.'

'We're going back to the clubhouse first,' Mama reminded them. 'We gotta get tooled up.'

They climbed on to their hogs, kicked them into snarling life and sped back to the canal.

Inside, Mama took a key from the chain hanging around her neck and opened up the 'armoury' ...an old brass-bound travelling trunk. Inside it were weapons of every description. She delved in, fishing out articles of war and distributing them around.

For herself, Mama chose a heavy set of steel knuckle-dusters, the top edges criss-crossed with tiny saw-cuts to make the face of the weapon even more destructive.

She handed out six pick-axe handles, a dozen flick-knives and several more sets of dusters. Lengths of heavy cycle chain were doled out like kiddies' sweets, and each Angel place a hog footrest in his pocket to serve as a small cosh.

As a final armament, Mama handed each Angel in turn six small yellow pills.

She held out a helping to Juice, who shook his head slowly.

'Not for me, Mama...I'll take my speed the quick way.' He nudged Julie in the ribs with his elbow.

'Give us the goodies, babe.'

Julie fished dutifully in her handbag and pulled out a slim black case which looked as though it had been made to hold spectacles.

Opening it, Juice pulled out the small hypodermic syringe and cupped it lovingly in his hand. He rammed the needle through the rubber stopper on the tiny bottle of clear liquid Julie held out, and sucked the precious amphetamine up into the syringe.

He rolled up his sleeve, exposing the small line of red marks which snaked up his arm. Finding a comparatively clear section of flesh, he stuck the needle in slowly and carefully, probing for a vein. He pushed the plunger down gently, whipped out the syringe and wiped it carefully on a piece of tissue.

Julie took it back and carefully replaced it in the case.

'Now remember Juice...you stay well clear of the action,' Mama reminded him.

He stared at her glassy-eyed, a stupid grin stealing across his face.

'Don't worry about me, Mama,' he slurred. 'With this stuff in me I can't feel a frigging thing.'

'OK. Pretty Boy,' Mama called out. 'We're following you.'

They poured out of the clubhouse and mounted the hogs.

'We'll make the battle of the Khyber Pass look like a tea party.' swore Mama before they blasted off on their errand of revenge.

CHAPTER NINE

THE RAID

Pretty Boy Parritt led the small band of avenging Angels towards their target like a homing pigeon. Down the Pentonville Road roared the twenty-four hogs, along Whitechapel and along the main road towards Stepney.

Close on his tyre tracks came Mama, her face set in a grim smile as she conjured with images of the mayhem and violence ahead of them. Tonight she felt good - glad to be out on a mission of violence, glad to have the chance to hate. The small numbers gave her a feeling of power, as though she realised that she led a tiny, but invincible army of guerrillas into warfare. There was more kick than in leading a massed rally of Hells Angels...perhaps it was something to do with being a big fish in a small pool.

Anyway, she felt that tonight would give her an important chance to show real class.

She rode hard, taking sharp corners recklessly and forcing Pretty Boy to keep his pace slightly ahead of her. Behind, the others followed as best they could, occasionally getting strung out along the road when they negotiated a particularly difficult bend.

Juice brought up the rear, struggling with the heavy hog despite the tearing pains which ripped through his side. The drugs helped - but not enough to deaden the effects of his injuries. Only the spirit of revenge kept him going.

Pretty Boy flung up one arm and slewed the hog into the kerb.

'It's just round the next block,' he shouted as the Angels pulled up behind him.

'OK. We'd better have some plan of action,' said Mama, taking the initiative once again.

'Danny, Pretty...you come with me. We'll go take a quick shufti. The rest of you stay here for a while.'

The three scouts peeled away from the kerb and cruised round the corner.

'There it is,' said Pretty Boy, pointing to a brightly coloured building halfway up the street. 'That's where they meet - in there.'

Mama glanced towards the building - a hastily converted

church hall. The outside had been painted bright pink, with violent blue stripes over the tops of the doors and windows.

There was not much activity. The street was practically deserted.

The three Angels cruised over to the hall warily, their engines merely ticking over.

As they approached Mama could hear the faint strains of sitar music filtering out into the street.

'Sounds like they're having a party,' she mumbled to Danny. He nodded.

'We ought to give 'em a nice little party surprise,' he muttered nastily.

'Look - there's a Paki kid,' whispered Pretty Boy, pointing to the far end of the street.

Mama strained her eyes. 'Can't see the bastards in the dark,' she cursed under her breath.

'Yeah, I see him,' said Danny after a second or two. 'Reckon we ought to watch him for a minute?'

'Go get him,' snapped Mama quickly. 'Grab the little sod before he sees us and gets in to warn the others.' As she spoke, the Paki kid looked towards them and froze in his tracks. He paused for only a second before breaking into a run.

Quick as a flash, Danny was away after him. The hog flew down the road like an arrow, closing in on the kid and cutting him off from the safety of the community centre.

As Danny loomed over him, the kid opened his mouth to shout. A swinging length of cycle chain across the top of his head shut him up before he uttered a sound. Danny paused only to prop up his hog, sling the kid across the back of the pillion and streak back up the road.

'Let's get back round the corner,' snapped Mama, and took off to spin the Harley round in the road.

They returned to the waiting gang.

'Hey, what's this...taking prisoners of war?' asked Superspade jokingly, as he set eyes on the unconscious kid.

'Thought we'd ask the little swine a few questions,' said Mama, parking the Harley and striding over to the kid.

She lifted him off the bike by his hair. Barely conscious,

the kid winced with pain and fell to the pavement.

The Angels looked down at him. He was no more than fourteen, but already conditioned to the tough life he had to live in the East London ghetto district. Tucked into the waistband of his trousers was a wicked-looking knife, and heavy metal blakeys had been driven into the front of his boots.

He looked up at his captors with frightened brown eyes. He just stared, the whites of his eyes rolling around and showing against the dark, swarthy skin of his face. He said nothing.

'OK you dirty little wog,' snapped Mama, twisting on the kid's hair again. 'Where's all your tough little mates then? Inside the monkey-house, are they?'

The kid still didn't answer. Mama gave his thick hair a vicious tug and he screamed out with pain.

'Talk, you lousy little bastard,' she hissed angrily.

The kid broke into an excited babble of sing-song pidgin English.

'The little bugger doesn't even speak English,' muttered Danny the Deathlover in disgust.

'Ahh - he's bluffing,' said Mama, and pressed her foot across the kid's throat, driving it against the pavement. 'Talk English, you little bastard, before you choke to death.'

The kid gagged, fought for air and tried to scream...but still didn't make any sense.

'I guess you're right,' Mama admitted at last. 'He doesn't speak English.' She released her booted foot, giving the kid a chance to claw for air.

'So what we gonna do with him?' asked Pretty Boy Parritt. 'The minute we let him go, he'll run right in there and warn his buddies.'

Mama motioned to Juice. He cruised over slowly.

'Here's your chance to do something useful, Juice,' she said. 'Take this kid as far away as possible and dump him. Turn the little bastard into curry if you want to.'

A wicked grin crossed Juice's face.

'Only too happy to oblige,' he snarled, and kicked the kid across the side of the head to put him to sleep again. The movement cost him a shriek of agony as his injured side tore against the fresh stitches. He looked over his shoulder to

70

Julie.

'Hop off, babe,' he muttered. She obliged quickly, bending down to help Mama pick up the kid and drape him across the pillion.

'Watch how you go,' warned Mama as he made to roar off. 'We don't want him falling off at speed and killing himself.'

Juice laughed nastily. 'Run these bunnies over and they just fill up the holes in the tarmac,' he shouted back. 'Their peepers make good cats eyes for a dark night.'

However, he cruised off carefully, making sure that his passenger was not thrown off by any sudden acceleration.

'OK...now here's what we're gonna do,' Mama started to explain as her band gathered thickly around her. 'The best chance we got is to strike fast and use surprise tactics. Now either we can draw 'em out into the street or we can go in there after them.'

'But we don't know how many of 'em there are in there,' pointed out Mudso nervously. 'They might beat the living hell out of us.'

Mama sneered at him

'Getting chicken, Muds?' she jeered. 'Maybe you wanna ride home and watch the TV instead?'

Mudso shuffled awkwardly.

'I was only mentioning it,' he mumbled under his breath.

'As I was saying,' Elaine continued patiently. 'We can go in, or try to get 'em in the street. Now, to my way of thinking, they've got a better chance in the street. They can scatter, gang up or they can get to damage the hogs.'

As she mentioned the hogs, her Angel followers muttered ominously.

'Yeah...you hadn't thought of that, had you?' Mama threw at them '...So I reckon we'd be better off going straight in there and giving 'em the works on their home ground.'

'Yeah. That sounds best,' agreed Danny the Deathlover. 'Yeah.'

Mama cast him a cynical smile.

'As long as you agree, Danny, that's all we need,' she said sarcastically. 'Now, shall we get on with some action and quit all this fart-assing about?'

'What about the hogs?' asked Grass.

'Leave 'em here...the birds can stick around and keep a look-out for trouble,' Mama answered him. She climbed off the big Harley and checked her armaments carefully.

'Just one thing,' she reminded them. 'As soon as we get in there, just hit out first and ask questions afterwards...OK?'

Mama led the way round the corner and towards the target. The gang bunched up around her, flicking cautious glances from side to side as they walked. The sense of nervousness was still strong amongst them. There was the strong possibility that they would be badly outnumbered, the area was not a 'safe' one for them at the best of times. They were playing an away game - and the local supporters could be an ugly bunch.

The door to the community centre was open. Mama pushed it gently and peered inside. The sounds of the Indian music swelled out into the quiet street. Inside, a long passageway led straight to a door which was closed. All the activity was behind that door.

The Angels crowded into the entrance hall and crept quietly down the passage. Mama paused in front of the door, her hand stretched out to almost grasp the handle.

'Right' she screamed, grabbing the handle and twisting it. 'Let the mothers have it!' She flung open the door and rushed in, with her gang close on her heels.

She took in the occupants of the room in one hasty glance, and an evil grin spread across her face as she took in the blur of puzzled, frightened faces. It was much better than she had imagined. There were perhaps fifty people in the hall...many of them middle-aged and a lot of them mere kids of thirteen or so. The actual number of young toughs was quite low - and in any case, the Angels had the advantage of surprise.

Trusting her followers to sort themselves out, Mama made straight for the small stage, upon which two young sitar players had suddenly paused in their recital. She ran through the aisle between the neatly-lined chairs and jumped up on the stage with one flying leap.

It was like taking white sticks from blind men. The Pakistanis were petrified with fear and surprise. The Angel's initial attack resembled a gang of hoodlums destroying a wax museum.

With a swinging kick, Mama's booted foot connected with one of the delicate sitars, sending it clattering across the stage with its strings singing a discordant jangle. The owner rose from his seat as though to go in rescue, but Mama reached out, grasped him round the neck and pushed him roughly towards the edge of the stage. She had learned well from Superspade - learned the judo techniques of using the opponent's weight and inertia as a weapon against him. The movement up from the chair gave him a forward impetus which Mama followed. The push sent him to the edge of the stage where he collapsed on to his knees and dived headfirst over the edge. When the top of his head made contact with the bare wooden floor, he promptly forgot all about retaliation.

Mama jumped towards the fallen sitar and stamped heavily upon it. The thin wood splintered and cracked open, and the tension of the strings did the rest. The instrument folded up into a wreckage which would never play another note.

She turned to face the hall and quickly assessed the situation. There was no doubt that the Angels were in complete control of the situation. Groups of the more nervous Pakistanis had bunched up in the corners of the room, seeking protection from the havoc all around them. Those who had chosen to put up a fight were being systematically tackled by Angels in groups of three - one facing them and two attacking from behind.

Grass was waving one of the metal-framed chairs above his head, smashing it down on every black head he could see.

Mama smiled happily and paused to glance down at the heavy brass knuckle-duster on her right fist. She adjusted it, clenched the fist and jumped from the stage into the general melee with her arm swinging. She moved towards Pretty Boy, who was swinging his heavy pick-axe handle at brown ankles like a scythe. As the victims doubled up with the pain, Mama was right there to slice the sharp knuckle-dusters across their faces and heads. Her hand was soon red with blood.

At the back of the hall, Adolph had discovered a padlocked cupboard and was trying to prise it open with a tyre lever.

Successful at last, the door burst open and gymnasium and games equipment tumbled out on to the floor.

Adolph produced a flick-knife from his pocket and set about the methodical destruction of the equipment. He sliced footballs into ribbons, slashed the soles of plimsolls and ripped table-tennis nets into shreds. Only when he had reduced the contents to the cupboard to a pile of useless rubbish did he pause in his labours.

He looked up just in time. A large Pakistani youth, tearing himself free from the clutches of two other Angels, sprang towards him with a scream of fury. Adolph turned to face him as the youth rushed forwards. He thrust out his arm in self defence...and the knife was still in his hand.

With a horrible scream, the Pakistani impaled himself upon the outstretched blade. It sank into the soft gut beneath his ribs up to the hilt. His lanky body jack-knifed, his legs seemed to turn to jelly beneath him and he sank to the floor with a look of wild fear in his dark brown eyes. He lay there, looking up, and the whites of his eyes burned like fire.

Adolph looked down at him, half-stunned by the speed at which it had all happened. They stared at the accusing hilt of the knife protruding from the youth's stomach in fascinated horror. A thick pool of blood had already started to puddle out on to the floor.

Mama rushed across the room, took one look down at the injured Pakistani and grabbed Adolph by the arm.

'Get the hell out of here,' she hissed quickly, pushing him towards the door.

Adolph obeyed dumbly, pausing at the door to look back in awe at the bleeding youth.

'Go on - get moving...we'll see you back at the hogs in a minute.' With a second push, she sent Adolph running down the passageway towards the door.

'Grass...Danny...get the boys together,' she screamed across the room above the noise of the fray.

Danny the Deathlover backed towards her, clubbing out from side to side with a pick-axe handle as he crossed the room. He reached her side, and looked over his shoulder to where the injured youth lay in his little pool of gore.

'We'd better get out right now,' he said with alarm in his voice.

'Yeah - when we've finished,' agreed Mama coldly. 'But before we leave, I want this place smashed to a pulp.'

She pointed towards the windows.

'Smash 'em,' she commanded curtly. Then, gesturing towards a collection box mounted on the wall ...'Get the bread out of that.'

Danny glanced at her nervously.

'Come on, Mama - let's just get out of here fast,' he said, glancing once again at the stabbed youth.

'Do what you're told, Danny,' snapped Mama curtly. 'Tell the boys to finish up what we came here to do.'

She picked up a heavy china Buddha from a nearby shelf and flung it at the nearest window. The glass shattered into the street outside.

Danny stared at her for a moment, seeing the fire which burned in her eyes. A thoughtful frown crossed his face for just a moment. Finally, he shrugged, and half-heartedly picked up a steel-framed chair and swung it at the collection box. Plaster showered to the floor as the blow knocked the box clean out of the wall. Danny bent down and deftly prised open the box with a tyre lever. Scooping up the meagre collection of assorted coins, he bundled them into his pockets and turned his attention to helping a nearby colleague fight off two enraged Pakis.

Mama moved towards the remaining windows, grasping at the thick curtains which hung from the ornate decorated pelmets. She tugged, bringing the material cascading to the floor in an untidy heap. Her sharpened knuckle-dusters soon ripped the expensive curtains to shreds. A handy chair soon put paid to the remaining glass.

She turned, looked around for more targets with a flushed smile on her face. Above her head, a delicate chandelier hung, shimmering from the ceiling. She reached out to her side, where Pretty Boy clubbed out wildly with his axe handle. Snatching it from his clasp she pushed him roughly aside.

'Look out,' she screamed at the top of her voice and

75

stretched upwards to swing at the chandelier. A small circle quickly cleared around her as her intention became more obvious.

Mama swung viciously, jumping back out of the way as a shower of chattered crystal poured from the smashed chandelier.

She looked around again. There was nothing breakable remaining.

'OK,' she screamed loudly. 'We're getting out...make for the door.'

She turned and ran straight for the exit.

Two young Pakis sidled round her to block off her escape. Mama anticipated their move and picked up a chair as she ran. Nearing them, she jumped sideways, distracting their attention from the escape route they guarded and made a feint with the chair. As the two youths hovered in indecision, she threw it at their heads and dived straight towards the door as they jumped aside. One of the youths tried to tackle her, but he was a split second too late. Her weighted fist slammed into his groin, convulsing him with sudden agony. Then Mama was through the door and running up the hallway towards the street.

Behind her, the noise of fighting stopped abruptly as the Angels turned to run. Danny the Deathlover and Pretty Boy Parritt ducked out under cover of four Angels, dragging an unconscious comrade between them. They backed through the door fighting a rearguard action and made for the street.

It was over. The Pakistanis seemed content to let them go, apart from a few brave youngsters who tried to continue the fight. Most stayed where they were, watching their attackers disappear and thanking their lucky stars it was finished.

Danny slapped the face of the injured Angel, who seemed to revive slightly in the cool evening air. He stumbled groggily after his fleeing companions as they headed for the hogs.

It was a clean, quick getaway. The hogs streaked away into the night with a concerted roar of power. The entire operation had lasted only twenty minutes.

Mama led the way back to the Matlock Arms. Violence and mayhem behind them, the Angels had a clear hour left in which to enjoy the liquid spirits of Christmas. A couple of times she glanced over her shoulder at Adolph, who rode close behind her. His face was ashen, and set into a hard, grim mask. Mama wondered vaguely whether the Paki had been killed. The knife wound had looked pretty bad and there had been a lot of blood. They'd soon know, she reminded herself. It wouldn't take the fuzz too long to pick them up once they had the descriptions to go on. That was if the fuzz ever got to hear about it. If the kid lived, the chances were that the Pakistani community would contain the event within itself...cops weren't too welcome when they could so easily poke their blue noses into nasty little affairs like illegal papers, local protection rackets and other minor troubles which the immigrant community shared.

Mama glanced once more at Adolph's shocked expression and mentally marked him down as a kid likely to turn yellow if the going was tough. His class rating dropped to zero.

Back at the Matlock, Juice's grinning, glazed face greeted them as they strolled in.

'What took you so long?' he joked.

Mama smiled back at him.

'Consider yourself well revenged,' she muttered under her breath. Peter the publican was hovering sneakily around with his ears wide open. Scraps of information came in useful when the fuzz bothered him. A little bit of grass kept pigs well fed for a month.

'What happened to the kid?' Mama asked.

A huge grin cracked across Juice's face.

'I got a little souvenir,' he said. 'Look!' Delving into his pockets, he produced a thick handful of black, greasy hair.

'I scalped the little bastard with a blade,' he explained with a laugh. 'You should have heard the little sod scream.'

Mama looked at the shorn hair and laughed. The mental picture of a bald-headed Paki kid crossed her mind and amused her greatly.

'You'd better dump it,' she murmured after a while. 'It's possible that the fuzz may come chasing.'

Juice's smile faded. 'What happened?' he asked seriously.

'Adolph stuck a blade in some kid - it looked pretty bad,'

Mama whispered quietly.

Juice fingered his injured side reflectively.

'Serve 'em right,' he spat with venom. 'Good for Adolph.'

He crossed the pub to Adolph, who stood alone in the corner.

'Well done, mush,' he chuckled, clapping his arm around Adolph's shoulders.

Adolph shrugged it off testily and edged away. 'It was an accident,' he hissed from between gritted teeth. He still looked rattled.

'Ha!' exclaimed Juice with another grin. 'Them bastards are accidents from the moment they're born. Don't worry about it, kid.'

'Come on - let's get some booze into us,' shouted Mama from the bar. 'This one's on the treasury.'

The crowd of Angels jostled the bar gratefully, calling out their orders.

They talked in excited voices, touched up their birds and slung down pints thirstily.

There was an hour of pub time left, there was money in their pockets and they'd had a ball.

It was a happy Christmas all round.

CHAPTER TEN

GREAT AMERICAN DREAM

Mama, Juice James, Julie and Ethel sat moodily in the clubhouse and played old rock and roll records.

It was a quiet night - although many nights had been quiet recently.

Too damned quiet.

Outside, early March had kept true to its tradition of coming in like a lion. A harsh wind howled down the alleyways alongside the canal, and the rain beat upon the corrugated steel roof of the clubhouse.

Things were changing within the Angels - and they were changing for the worse, reflected Elaine bitterly.

'Don't look like no one's gonna turn up tonight,' said Ethel to no one in particular.

'Shitty night, ain't it?' muttered Juice, as though absolving everyone from blame. He glanced towards Elaine.

'What d'ya reckon?'

It was a pointless question, meaning nothing at all. In the moody depression which hung over them all, it merely pressed for conversation.

'I don't reckon much at all,' Mama replied with a bored shrug of her shoulders. 'Except that if I don't get up off my arse this minute I'm gonna put down roots.'

She jumped to her feet irritably, crossed the clubhouse and helped herself to a can of beer from the stores. Deftly pulling back the ring opener, she poured the light ale down her throat greedily.

'Anybody wanna beer?'

Juice and Ethel waved their hands in the air feebly.

'Here - catch.' Mama threw two cans across the room in quick succession. She returned to the group and sank down once again on the mattress. A stony silence descended once again, broken only by the sound of rain hammering upon the roof.

'Jeezus - what a crappy country this is,' observed Juice after a while. 'Just listen to that friggin' rain!'

'Yeah - I can hear it,' remarked Mama sarcastically. She fumbled on the floor beside her mattress and picked up a discarded dog-eared paperback book.

'Anyone read this?' she asked, flipping through the pages moodily.

'Yeah - I brought it in,' said Juice. 'It's good stuff.'

Mama glanced at the title - 'Rebel Wheels' - and the cover picture of a motorcycle gang riding across desert sands.

'It's a bit of a hype really,' confessed Juice, sensing Mama's initial disapproval. 'I mean - it's written by some guy who claims to ride with the Angels in the States, but I reckon he's probably just an ordinary, uptight citizen who made some quick bread out of it...but, Man some of the descriptions of all that road and all that country to run in...Man, it's the end!'

Mama's eyes misted over as she thought about it.

'Yeah,' she muttered dreamily. 'It must be something else to have a hog with a full tank and a coupla thousand miles of nothing but highway ahead of you.'

'Easy rider,' muttered Juice happily. 'Wow, what a trip!'

'Just think,' Mama continued, her eyes ablaze with wild imagination. 'In one run, you can go through cities, towns and even miles of bloody desert. Christ! It makes you realise what a pissy little island we live on, don't it?'

'Yeah. Them Yanks have got a beautiful scene,' agreed Juice, his voice tinged with awe and envy. 'Man - one day, I'm gonna get me over there with a hog and a wad of bread...and then I'm just gonna keep on riding till I drop.'

'Well, why don't we just do exactly that?' said Mama suddenly. Juice stared at her blankly.

'How do you mean?'

'You know - blow over to the States for a long trip. Shit, all we need is a bit more bread.'

Juice stared at her coolly for a few seconds. Finally he let a slow whistle out through his teeth.

'Jeeze...you really mean it, don't your?' he asked.

'Yeah. Why not?' Mama responded excitedly. 'We could write to one of the big Angel chapters over there, tell 'em we was coming, and I bet they'd have a reception committee waiting for us. Just think, Man, we could run down to Mexico, California...just about any damn where.'

Juice could only shake his head slowly from side to side in disbelief.

'Man! What a trip,' he echoed blankly. Then, coming briefly down to harsh realities, his face fell. 'It'd take a helluva lot of bread, Mama.'

'So we pull off a really big job,' Mama shot back immediately. 'Just one really nice piece of work...quit all this frigging around with peanuts and pull off a one-time bonanza. Christ, Juice...we could make a couple of thousand quid - maybe more - to take us just about anywhere we wanted to go.'

'Great idea, but we just ain't got the organisation for that sort of thing,' Ethel put in soberly.

Juice glared at him, his face became deadly serious.

'He's right,' he murmured sadly to Mama. 'We couldn't do anything like that...Christ, some of the boys is already beginning to chicken out.'

'That's just what's wrong at the moment,' snapped Mama. 'Look at us here tonight. Christ Almighty, a month ago there'd have been twenty or thirty sitting around here and having a ball. Now what...one night of rain and they all stay in to watch the fugging picture-box.'

'You been pushing 'em a bit heavy, Mama,' Julie muttered reprovingly. 'A lot of the boys feel that you been taking everything a bit too serious...know what I mean?'

'Gutless bastards,' spat Mama viciously. 'Half of the yellow-gutted mothers just want to piss around on hogs and get cheap thrills. Fuck it, I offered 'em the chance to really be something...you know? Without me, they're just kids with a motorbike between their legs...Christ, since I took over, we're really somewhere - we got half this manor eating out of our hands. If I had a bit more enthusiasm, I could make the Hells Angels into a real power-force.'

'Maybe they don't want to be a power, Mama,' said Ethel quietly. 'Maybe they just want to be kids, and blast off a little steam sometimes. I mean, it ain't really worth all the hassle, is it?'

'Oh, come on Man, don't you catch the disease as well,' Mama chided him. 'Are you forgetting what we are? We're the Hells Angels, Ethel...we're a different breed - a group apart from those pigs out there.' She waved a hand vaguely towards the clubhouse door. 'We gotta show them just how different we are...we gotta make the bastards see that the Angels is really something to reckon with. You forgetting all that, Man?'

'No, I'm not forgetting where we're at,' said Ethel in a quiet, withdrawn voice. 'But maybe you're starting to forget, Mama. Maybe you're just trying to make 'em what they ain't, and what they don't want to be.'

'OK - then they can drop out. We don't need them,' Mama snapped angrily.

'...And that's exactly what they ARE doing,' put in Ethel quietly. He gestured around the empty clubhouse. 'See for yourself.'

Mama digested his words soberly. She sat quietly, thinking over the past months and putting things together.

It had all seemed so easy, so straightforward. There had been a disorganised rabble, lacking a leader and a common purpose. She had become that leader, given them a unifying purpose, and the rabble had been transformed into an organised gang. They had everything going for them, and no worries. All they had to do was to follow orders. They didn't even have to think for themselves. Big Mama did all that sort of thing for them.

Elaine thought of her own immediate followers. Sure, there had been bitching, a little bit of resentment. A few Angels had dropped out along the line when they couldn't take her orders any more. Some had chickened - like Adolph after the stabbing affair with the Pakis. But there had been new, eager young blood coming in as well, there had been Danny the Deathlover's devotion to her and his strong right arm to pull others into line behind him. Freaky, Max the Knife, Superspade, Pretty Boy, Irish Mick...and a dozen others, all right behind her all the way.

...Only they weren't behind her right now. Even Danny hadn't been around for nearly a week now.

Anger, and then resentment welled up inside her.

'Ungrateful bastards,' she said out loud.

Juice and Ethel looked at her in surprise.

Julie moved forwards to put a consoling arm around her shoulders.

'We'll sort 'em out,' she said confidently. 'You leave it to Juice and me.'

Mama laughed sarcastically. 'Great bloody leader I am,' she said bitterly. 'Got to leave the sorting out to other people.'

'Look, Mama, don't take it so personal,' said Juice, sensing Elaine's general air of despondency. 'You've done a bloody marvellous job - all of us know that, and...Hell...nobody really wants out. It's just that, well...I guess some of the boys didn't really go for the big crime scene, you know? I mean they want kicks, Mama...we been making it too much like a goddamn business...like going out and getting a job.'

'What about you, Juice?' Mama shot at him. She stared him coolly in the eyes.

Juice grinned recklessly.

'Shit, Mama,' he said. 'You know me...I'm ripe for anything.'

Mama glanced at Ethel, the same question in her eyes. She didn't say a word. There was no need to speak.

'I'm with you,' Ethel grunted. 'Hell, I'm getting too old to be a hothead kid anymore.'

'So how many we really got left?' asked Mama bluntly.

'All my boys are still behind me,' said Juice with great certainty. 'How about you, Man?'

Ethel shrugged off the direct question. 'Who knows?' he muttered vaguely. 'I reckon at least six of 'em would still choose to ride with me if they got the chance. Grass, definitely, would be in at the kill.'

He turned to look at Mama. She eyed the two men warily, sensing that it was her turn to shout heads.

'Maybe ten I could really count on,' she admitted ruefully. 'I'm pretty sure that Danny would come back into the fold without too much persuasion. I'm not quite sure how far he'd go, that's all. As for the rest, well I reckon Superspade would be in it just for the kicks, Freaky and Max would follow anyone who gave 'em an order, Pretty Boy and the rest are just wild enough to do anything as long as it promised them fun.'

A silence fell once again, as the four sat to digest the information and thoughts which had passed between them.

'So?' muttered Juice finally, as though awaiting a declaration of some sort.

'So how about it?' Mama responded. 'How about planning one really great, grand slam, splitting it and cutting out for the States?'

They considered the grand dream in all its shades of reality.

'It's worth thinking about,' admitted Ethel rather grudgingly.

'It's a beautiful idea,' murmured Julie dreamily.

'Well let's do something about it,' said Juice firmly. 'Let's just start to do something concrete.'

Mama smiled happily, her earlier depression wiped away by the sheer enthusiasm she had worked up.

'I'll write to the Californian chapters tonight,' she vowed. 'Right now, let's get out and chase a few more of the boys up...we got some pruning out to do.'

She rose, and led the way to the door.

'Where do we start looking?' asked Ethel.

'Nick the Greek's,' Mama shot back at him as she walked outside to the waiting Harley-Davidson. 'I'm betting ten to one a lot of the boys have gone back to hanging out there.'

She sat astride the hog and kicked it over. It coughed noisily a couple of times and finally spluttered into life.

'That hog sounds as though it could do with a going over,' shouted Ethel above the roar. Mama flashed him a quick, mean glance.

'Don't try to tell me where I'm at,' she spat angrily at him. 'I can take care of myself...and my hog.' She snapped the machine into gear and released the clutch with a jerk. The rear wheel spun, bit into the road and thundered off towards the Greek's.

Ethel looked after her for a while, shrugged, and waited for Juice to mount up.

'Greek's,' he called, by way of explanation. He moved away slowly, with deliberate, exaggerated cool. Juice cruised along beside him.

They were both quite deeply engrossed in similar thoughts.

Mama was right. The small, dingy cafe hadn't changed over the months, and neither had the clientele. Perhaps two dozen Angels were sitting around, still toying with half-drunk cups of coffee and queuing up to play the fruit machine. They were all young, most of them make-believe Angels who had chickened out when the system started to become a little too organised for them. Mama glanced around, took in the assembled throng and dismissed them one by one. There wasn't one rider she'd care to have beside her. It was as if they were another cult, another breed - left behind somewhere along the line as rejected material.

She turned to leave without fully stepping through the door. A few of the Angels saw her, waved expectantly and tried to sound enthusiastic.

Mama presented them with her back without acknowledging their existence. She returned to the hog and turned it round in the street just as Juice and Ethel cruised up.

'Anyone in there?' Juice wanted to know.

'A bunch of kids,' Mama snorted in disgust, and made to move off.

'Hold it a second,' Juice called to her, dismounted from his hog and strolling towards the door. He peered in to the cafe.

When he returned, there was a strange, distant smile playing about his face.

'That "bunch of kids" you referred to are Hells Angels, Mama,' he muttered almost reproachfully. 'You can't afford to get so far out of touch you dismiss them just like that. They're Angels, and if they look like just kids to you, then it's you who's wrong, not them. They're young, they're a bit wild and they love hogs, boozing, raising hell and a good fight. But basically they're just hot-spirited kids who want to be a bit different from every other kid in this boring, watered-down world of ours. You wanna keep the Hells Angels together, Mama, then you're gonna have to cool down a little. They want action, and they want kicks...but they don't want to become full-time villains. Hell, that's growing up too fast and pushing 'em in the wrong way.'

'So what about our plan?' Mama asked wistfully, brought down by Juice's harsh realities.

He grinned. 'Man, that's our bag, ain't it?' he said pointedly. 'We keep that part to ourselves...meanwhile, we gotta tread the shallow water in their depth.'

For a moment, Mama bristled defiantly, but the sheer logic of Juice's argument pierced her defences. She slumped resignedly. 'Yeah - maybe you're right,' she muttered.

'I think so,' murmured Juice with a wry smile. 'Now - shall we go in and meet the fans?'

He led the way to the door, and pushed it open for Mama to enter. Nick the Greek glared at her with undisguised malice as she strolled in. He could see his business dwindling again, and the falling profits ran through his mind like an accounting computer.

'All right you miserable mothers,' she called out across the cafe. 'We're riding tonight...any of you coffee-swillers still got hogs?'

The challenge was irresistible. The Angels started to scramble to their feet expectantly.

'Where we going, Mama?' several of them asked.

'We're gonna burn up the M1,' Mama informed them. 'Only we're gonna have a run with a difference. There's a ten pound prize for the first guy who gets back to the clubhouse with a Birmingham street sign for a souvenir.'

She glanced quickly at her watch.

'It's nine-fifteen now...anyone with a bit of class can be back by one o'clock,' she announced.

A wave of sudden interest swept through the cafe. This was the style of Angel activity they appreciated - sheer speed, pure thrills, and the added bonus of a prize worth competing for.

The Angels quickly got their wings together, downed the remains of their drinks and started to put on their crash helmets.

Mama grabbed Juice by the arm and pulled him back through the door.

'Come on, let's ride,' she shouted, jumping astride the Harley and kicking it into life. She screamed away from the kerb with Juice and Ethel close behind her. Seconds later, they heard the concerted roar of twenty other hogs screaming out their challenge into the night.

Mama headed for the Holloway Road, straight as an arrow for the route out on to the North Circular and the M1.

She gunned the Harley feverishly, hunching down over the handlebars in an attempt to get even more speed out of the hog. Behind her Juice tried desperately to keep up, hampered as he was by the extra weight of Julie on the pillion. Jamming back the throttle as far as it would go, he brought the hog alongside her for long enough to shout his message.

'Can't keep up this pace,' he screamed across above the din of the engines. 'You'll have to go on ahead.'

Mama glanced sideways briefly.

'Forget it,' she screamed back. 'Keep going and I'll explain later.'

She slackened off on her throttle slightly, allowing Juice to fall in behind her and reduce his speed. She threw one more quick glance over her shoulder. Ethel was keeping pace nicely about twenty yards behind them.

Satisfied, she turned her attention back to the road ahead. A hundred yards further ahead, a green traffic signal glimmered. As the hogs sped towards it, the light changed to amber.

Mama heard the choking roar from Juice's bike as he throttled back.

'Jump 'em,' she screamed at the top of her voice, gunning her own engine into an extra burst of speed. The Harley leapt forwards towards the crossroads.

Juice followed her lead, quickly revving his Thunderbird up again to recoup his lost speed. A blast of angry horns challenged the three riders as they crashed through the red light and under the railway bridge. Another three hundred yards and another set of traffic lights awaited them. The lights stayed green, changing a few seconds after they passed through.

Mama glanced back over her shoulder and grinned happily. They had gained at least two precious minutes on anyone following them.

She kept up the crippling pace through Archway and raced up Highgate Hill. Another set of red lights and a slight traffic block brought them to a halt for the first time. Juice took advantage of the brief pause to pull alongside Mama.

'Hell, Mama, I know we're racing...but you're pushing it,' he complained.

Mama grinned back at him.

'Keep it up for as long as you can,' she snapped back mysteriously. 'I got some plans.'

The conversation was cut off abruptly as the red and amber light gave them the clearance to weave round five cars ahead of them and streak off once again. They stopped again at the North Circular Road intersection.

'Come on, what's it about?' asked Juice. Ethel too had pulled alongside, and the same query was written across his face.

'OK,' Mama snapped. 'I'll tell you. First of all, we've got to burn up the M1 until we get to the M45 turn off to Coventry. I want plenty of distance between us and the bunch behind...'

Her voice cut off suddenly as the lights changed once again. She was off like a streak, slashing across the carriageway to take the outside lane for the approach to the motorway.

The three riders hurtled through the night for an hour, Mama

87

keeping up the fierce pace every second of the journey. Eventually, they came to the warning approach signs to the M45.

Mama led them across the motorway and off on to the Coventry and Birmingham road. A few miles farther, she waved Juice down frantically and slewed the hog into an empty lay-by.

She propped the Harley up on its footrest, swivelled in the saddle and turned to confront her curious comrades.

'Right then. I suppose I'd better tell you what you're in for,' she said slowly, with a mysterious smile on her face.

She fumbled with the straps of her Nazi helmet, pulling the headgear loose. Gathering up her hair in thick tresses, she stuffed them out of sight inside the helmet, pulled it back on and tightened the straps carefully.

'We're gonna pull a little caper,' Mama said triumphantly. 'Just to show us all how easy it is. Only this is gonna make a ten quid prize out of the treasury look like peanuts.'

As she spoke, Mama fished in her pockets and pulled out a grimy neckerchief. She tied it around her chin, then slid it up so that it covered the bottom half of her face. In the half light provided by their headlamps, she no longer looked like woman. She was just a figure on a motorcycle, identifiable only by the Hells Angels colours on her back.

'Put on masks like this,' she told Ethel and Juice, pointing to her own. 'If you got goggles, put 'em on.'

They obeyed her blindly, content to follow orders, but burning with curiosity for the full story to be revealed. Ethel tied a handkerchief around his face and put on a pair of night driving goggles he kept in the tool-box. Juice made do with an oily piece of rag he kept for wiping the hog.

'What about me?' asked Julie.

'Don't bother,' snapped Mama. 'You'll have to keep out of the way.'

'Look, just what in hell IS going on,' asked Juice in an exasperated voice. 'How long ya gonna keep us in suspense, Mama?'

Elaine laughed.

'In about half an hour from now, you'll know about it,' she teased. 'Meanwhile, we keep riding until we get off the motorway.'

Refusing to say more, she spun the Harley out on to the road again and took off like a rocket.

Obediently, Juice and Ethel pulled out after her and accelerated to catch her up.

They rode on in silence for several minutes.

The motorway ended, giving way to the dual carriageway of the A45. Mama kept riding, until the end of the motorway was about six miles behind them. She waved her companions down again and brought the hog to a halt.

'There it is,' she said, and pointed up the road to a small petrol station, ablaze with bright lights. 'That's our pigeon.'

She leaned over the side of the Harley, flipped open the toolbox and drew out a heavy tyre lever.

'Better tool up...just in case,' she told them. Ethel, fishing in his pocket, produced a pair of brass knuckles, which he slipped on carefully.

'Mama - I ain't doing another goddamned thing until you tell us what this is all about,' snapped Juice in tense anger.

'Oh, didn't I tell you?' asked Elaine sardonically. 'We're gonna knock over that filling station up there...that's all.'

Juice stared at her blankly, his mouth wide open with amazement.

'Mama - are you crazy?' he asked at length.

Elaine grinned good-naturedly.

'Not at all,' she affirmed. 'I'm just beginning to get smart.'

'But you can't just charge in there and hold the goddamned place up,' Juice protested vigorously. 'It's too bloody risky.'

'No risk at all,' Mama reassured him. 'I've had this worked out for a long time. Look...here's what we do...'

She explained the plan in full detail. Juice, Ethel and Julie listened intently, quite stunned by the suddenness of it all. When she had finished explaining, Mama sat back in her saddle and smiled proudly.

'Well?' she asked.

There was a short silence, broken eventually by a slow, soft whistle from Juice's lips.

'Woweee...I think we could damn well do it at that,' he murmured enthusiastically.

'Of course we can do it,' snapped Mama curtly. 'I told you...I got it all worked out.'

She glanced at Ethel for his agreement. He merely smiled. Taking it for full assent, Mama turned to Julie.

'OK love...you get off here, and stay out of sight until you see us drive in to the filling station...then you walk up on the road to the other side and wait for us...got it?'

Julie nodded her head.

'Yeah. I got it,' she said, clambering off Juice's pillion.

'OK then...here we go,' said Mama as she kicked the machine into gear.

'Best of luck,' called Julie after them as they cruised towards the bright lights of the filling station. Juice merely waved his left hand in the air by way of acknowledgement.

Mama led the way to the entrance of the garage. She peered carefully around the forecourt. It was deserted.

'OK...you both know what to do?' she hissed.

Juice and Ethel nodded their heads.

'OK...in you go...and don't forget to keep your backs turned as much as possible...and for Christ's sake don't let the attendant get a glimpse of your number plates.'

She peeled away from them both, slipping the Harley over on to the grass verge which ran around the perimeter of the petrol station forecourt. She coasted in a big circle, the Harley making only a gentle noise of tickover.

Ethel and Juice roared up towards the petrol attendant, revving their engines as much as possible.

They stopped outside the bright pool of light thrown by the pumps and the overhead fluorescent tubes. In this dark patch of shadow, it would be virtually impossible for the attendant to pick out the number plates accurately...even if he was looking for them.

...And there was no earthly reason why he should do so. Nothing in the least extraordinary was happening...just two motorcycles stopping at an all-night petrol station for juice...a common enough occurrence.

Juice blasted his horn.

The attendant stepped out of his little office and strolled towards them.

From behind him, hidden by the wall of the garage toilets stepped Mama, the heavy tyre lever in her hand.

She tripped lightly across the concrete of the forecourt, her footsteps drowned by the noise of the two roaring motorcycle engines.

As the attendant neared Ethel and Juice, they half-turned away from him, as if to unlock their fuel tanks. The Hells Angel symbols on their backs stood out plainly. The attendant would have to be blind to miss them.

He saw them all right! They were the last thing he saw from some little while.

Mama swung the tyre lever down across the back of his head with a sickening crunch. The poor guy just folded up in mid-step, collapsing upon the ground in an unconscious heap.

'Right...let's go,' shouted Mama, already sprinting towards the cash desk. She ran in to the office, punched open the till and quickly scooped out the contents. She wrapped up the notes into a thick bundle, which she stuffed into her top pocket. The silver she gathered up in handfuls, and passed to Ethel and Juice in turn. They filled their pockets quickly, then turned and ran back to the hogs.

Mama ran for hers, jumping astride and taking off without bothering to kick the footrest. She bounced across the grass, hit the road once again and accelerated to where Juice was just picking up Julie on the Birmingham side of the filling station.

'OK. Let's ride,' shouted Mama exultantly, and gunned the Harley into action. They streaked off down the road, leaving the garage far behind.

Mama flicked a look at her watch as they rode.

Two minutes flat...and the thick, comforting bundle in her top pocket told her it had been well worth it.

She overtook Ethel and Juice and led them at breakneck pace for six or seven miles. She gestured towards a crossroads a few hundred yards further along the road, and slowed to a crawl.

Turning the corner, she pulled up and let the hog tick over gently.

'Now we wait for a while,' she murmured.

They waited. Two, three...five minutes.

Juice twitched nervously.

'Come on, Mama...hadn't we better get out of here?' he asked impatiently.

'Not yet,' Mama said quietly, straining her ears for the sound she was waiting for.

Another minute passed...and then they all heard it.

The sound of a powerful motorcycle roaring up the main road towards them. The hog screamed past, followed only a second later by two more riders.

'OK...back to London,' muttered Mama with a triumphant smirk. '...Only WE'RE going back by a different route.'

She cruised away slowly, accelerating up to a comfortable speed in the sixties. There was no point in attracting unwanted police attention for speeding now.

They travelled down the side road, cutting through country lanes until they finally came out to a road which led back to the M1.

Mama looked at her watch again.

'OK,' she said. 'Even the last of the stragglers will have been past by now.' She led the way on to the approach road which filtered into the motorway and began the trek back to London.

Back in the clubhouse, they counted the night's takings.

'Jeezus,' exclaimed Juice, as they totted up just under two hundred quid. 'I wouldn't have thought a little place like that would take so much dough in a day.'

Mama smiled.

'Petrol's bloody expensive,' she reminded him. 'And that site is busy during the day.'

They sat for several minutes, gloating over the spoils, and drinking a celebrationary beer.

'Right, we'd better get the dough out of here,' said Mama at last, jumping to her feet. 'I expect a pretty bewildered fuzz will be round here soon enough, looking for a needle in a haystack.'

She thrust the money towards Julie.

'Here babe,' she said. 'You look after it for a while. You weren't even there.'

They all laughed. It was, after all, a gigantic joke. Mama could imagine the joy of the interviewing copper when the petrol attendant revealed that they had at least twenty suspects in the immediate area. It would take the local police all their time and facilities to swoop upon all the riders between London and Birmingham.

...And not one of them would be carrying the spoils. There

would be two dozen beautiful suspects but not one tiny shred of convicting evidence. The fuzz could suspect, but they'd never be able to prove a thing. Sheer numbers were counting in the Angel's favour. Meanwhile, the real culprits were sitting happily back in London, with the loot stashed well out of the way.

It was beautiful!

Mama crossed the clubhouse, and dug under a pile of old junk.

She fumbled around for a second, eventually producing the broken half of a cast-iron street name plate.

She held it up with a laugh.

'We even win the tenner,' she said. 'I picked this up in Small Heath a couple of months ago.'

Ethel and Juice roared with laughter. The joke was now perfect.

'OK...let's wait around for our boys or the fuzz...whoever gets here first,' she said.

Julie stood up to leave.

'I'll dump the dough,' she said quietly. 'Shall I come back?'

'Better not,' said Mama quietly. 'See you tomorrow.'

Julie bent to plant a kiss on Juice's cheek. 'See you, lover,' she said finally, and ducked out of the door.

'I vote we all have another drink,' said Ethel, and made his way towards the beer supplies.

They sat exultant, flushed with victory and the sheer thrill of beating the system and slowly got good and drunk.

CHAPTER ELEVEN

THE WAITING GAME

When the police investigations were finally over, and the CID had shelved the case in disgust, there were still plenty of suspicions floating around in the Angel circle. Many of those on the Birmingham run clearly suspected that they had been set up as prime suspects, but there was no proof, and their code kept them tight-lipped and together.

Mama, Juice, Ethel and Julie kept their secret well. Only a few, well-trusted Angels were in on the full story - and their reaction had been mixed, to say the least.

The general consensus of opinion was that it had been a worthwhile caper, purely from the point of view of outwitting the fuzz, but that the manner in which the operation had been conducted transgressed some of the more ethical Angel codes.

Danny the Deathlover's initial reaction had been one of disappointment. Somehow, his instinctive trust in Mama as the great saviour figure had been badly betrayed. He wished that things could go backwards, and perhaps recoup their original promise.

Danny was a Hells Angel to the core, and it upset him to see the fine organisation beginning to crumble away.

He had decided to stick around, hovering over Mama in his self-cast role of Father protector...and yet he could even see this tenuous position being sucked away from him by Juice James.

Juice had managed to gain Mama's complete confidence. She, in turn, had responded to him in a way she had never been willing to respond to Danny. Perhaps, because he had Julie as his old lady, Mama felt a certain sense of security...he represented no sexual threat to her omnipotence.

Whatever the reason, Danny was willing to play a waiting game - hoping that things would get better, but preparing himself to be on the spot to pick up some of the pieces when the big crunch came.

Mama too was playing her own version of the waiting game. The ease of the petrol station job had enthused her, and she was already living out her dreams down those long, bleak American superhighways. The Hells Angels had provided her with a rough framework upon which to construct her dreams, and she did not want to dismantle the foundations...not yet, anyway. While she could retain their interest and maintain her control over them, she was still in a position to make bigger plans.

...So, for the moment, the status quo had been restored and was being kept in running order. The Angels were reasonably united once again, and their leader was calling the shots.

Mama had seen the danger light, and was giving them what they wanted. Right now, it was Saturday afternoon, and the word was out for a run.

Danny the Deathlover looked round the clubhouse and made a count of heads. There had been a lot of thinning out, but most of the regular faces were in evidence.

Danny checked over the crowd again, trying to identify and assess the small, hard core which was beginning to make itself evident.

There was Juice James, and his satellite group of four...Soapy, Little Ed, Dirty Dick and Ringo. They were hard characters, older than most Angels, and nearer the gang-member image which Mama seemed to be admiring in recent months.

Ethel's immediate followers included Trucker, Sam the Spick and Grass, but Danny suspected that only Ethel would be at Mama's side when the chips were down.

Of the original group, only he, Freaky, Pretty Boy Parritt and Max the Knife were still truly close to Mama - but Danny felt sure that they all shared his reservations about the future. Some of the younger bloods - new members like Superspade and two more negro Angels he had brought in to the circle - affected an air of total subservience to Mama's will. They were new enough to still be slightly awe-struck, grateful for the honour of Angelhood and eager to prove class.

Danny wondered, vaguely, just how much Mama trusted her followers now. He couldn't help but suspect that she was relying on her power too much. If trouble struck, she might easily find herself out on a limb with no help at all.

It was an unpleasant thought, stirring all of Danny's protective instincts towards Elaine - but there was so little he could do to help matters.

Danny turned his back on the assembled horde and strolled outside to get some of the watery sunshine which March had to offer. He stood just outside the door, paused and pensively lit a cigarette. His eyes roved over the clutter of parked hogs, finally alighting on Mama's big Harley-Davidson.

He sighed grimly once again. It bore yet more tell-tale signs of her gradual withdrawal from everything the Angels stood for. The once-gleaming chromium was dull. It hadn't been polished for weeks. The engine was mucky, splattered with oil stains and a coating of splashed mud.

He walked slowly towards it, fishing in the back pocket of his jeans for a piece of torn rag he always carried with him. Stooping over Mama's hog, he gently wiped some of the surface dirt away and tried to restore a gleam to the chromium. It was a labour of unrequited love.

Back inside the clubhouse, Mama looked around proudly at the massed rally. The same old exuberance which invariably preceded a run was there, and the babble of conversation was liberally spiked with laughter, merriment and enthusiasm.

Juice detached himself from his own small group and strolled towards her. As ever, Julie trotted obediently at his heels.

'Could be a nice run,' he mumbled conversationally. 'Good turnout.'

Mama nodded without speaking.

'Got any definite plans?' he went on.

Mama shrugged carelessly.

'Bournemouth, I thought,' she said, with a query in her voice.

'Yeah...great,' enthused Juice, giving her the encouragement she seemed to be asking for. 'We'll have a ball.'

He looked at her carefully. Mama seemed distant, withdrawn.

'Got something on your mind?' he asked.

There was a tiny sparkle buried deep in Elaine's blue eyes.

'I'm still thinking about it,' she said mysteriously, and Juice recognised the same dreamlike mischief she had displayed on the night of the filling station robbery. He grinned widely.

'You got something up your sleeve, haven't you?' he asked her directly.

Mama hedged away from the question with a non-committal nod of her head.

'Maybe,' she said. 'I'll let you know when it gels.'

'Find a part for me in the next one,' put in Julie, who had been listening attentively. 'That last caper was a dead loss as far as I was concerned.'

Mama smiled at her warmly.

'Yes...I might just do that,' she replied thoughtfully, and returned to the private thoughts in her head.

Juice glanced round the clubhouse. Only a few scattered riders had shown up for the last half-hour. It seemed as though the crowd was as large as it was likely to become. There was a certain nervous tension beginning to build up. The Angels were starting to get impatient.

'Reckon it's about time to run?' he asked Mama, deliberately making it a question, not a statement.

Mama snapped out of her reverie and followed his eyes around the clubhouse.

'Yeah...it's time,' she confirmed, starting to stroll towards the door.

'OK...we ride,' she shouted over her shoulder, and the crowd behind her cheered approvingly.

Mama walked slowly towards her hog. She stared at it, and a small frown creased her forehead as she noted the effects of Danny's little clean-up. She glanced sideways curiously. Danny was lounging against the side of his own hog several yards away. Their eyes met for a few seconds, and the tiniest flicker of recognition burned in Mama's eyes for a fraction of a second.

She turned away from him abruptly.

'We're hitting Bournemouth,' she shouted as she sat astride the Harley. 'Usual route out to the A30.'

Kicking over the hog, she sat astride it with the engine throbbing gently as the rest found their machines and mounted up. With an ear-splitting roar, the run commenced.

CHAPTER TWELVE

BIRDS OF A FEATHER

Mama rode grimly, occasionally glancing over her shoulder to admire the long phalanx of riders strung out behind her. They were fifty or sixty strong - a comfortable turnout by any standards, yet somehow the sight failed to trigger off any deep feelings of excitement. Once, such a sight would have filled her with pride and elation. Now, a small, but vital spark of interest was missing.

A run was just a run...there was nothing new about it, nothing powerful enough to stir the chill of fear and the fire of excitement in her stomach. Mama had tasted real power and the criminal kick...already she was addicted to it.

She rode skilfully, yet somehow detached from her own actions. As though on an automatic pilot, the Harley streaked in a straight line along the road, and hugged it tightly round the sharp bends. Mama's eyes were on the road ahead, but her mind was somewhere else.

After an hour's hard riding, Mama slowed down for the transport cafe she knew to be a mile or so farther up the road. Approaching it, she waved down her followers and peeled off the road on to the lorry park.

Juice pulled alongside her as she stopped.

'Hey - it's a bit early to make a stop, ain't it?' he queried, looking at Mama with a puzzled expression.

'We ain't stopping,' Mama hissed quietly. 'I just wanted to point this place out to you and Ethel. Pass the word on to your boys...discreetly mind...that we're meeting back here on the run back from Bournemouth. I don't care how you do it, just make sure we split up and get away from the main bunch on the way back. Tell Ethel to do the same.'

Juice looked over the transport cafe carefully, filing it away in his mind for future reference. It wasn't a big place, but there were ten or twelve large lorries parked outside and virtually no private cars.

He looked over his shoulder at the main bunch of Angels who had crowded up behind them. They sat astride their hogs, pulling back their throttles impatiently. The looks on the faces confirmed Juice's fears that they weren't too happy with the stop. They wanted to get to their target as quickly as possible.

His eyes flickered back to meet Mama's.

'OK....I'll pass the word,' he muttered.

She smiled. Then, turning the Harley round, she addressed her followers.

'Sorry fellers,' she shouted with an apologetic smile. 'I thought I had some petrol feed trouble...but it's OK. Let's get riding.'

She revved up, leading the small army back on to the road. They continued their journey towards Bournemouth, and hell-raising.

As raids went, Bournemouth could be considered to be a highly-honoured town. It was too close to London, and too popular with various gangs of suedeheads, Angels, and young tearaways on scooters. For over ten years, the people of Bournemouth had seen the Mods and the Rockers, the Agroboys and the skinheads, suedeheads, Greasers and the Hells Angels.

The names of the various gangs had changed over the years, but the pattern of violence and destruction remained the same.

Constant exposure to such attacks had taught the local police several grim lessons. Nowadays, they were more than equipped to deal with such outbreaks.

As the first wave of riders approached the outskirts of the town, the Panda cars were ready.

They didn't intercept...there was nothing to be gained from provoking a clash. Instead, they waited in lay-bys, parked by the side of roads and lurked prominently in side-streets.

They were just THERE...as visual reminders that trouble would be swiftly dealt with.

The Angels couldn't help but get the message.

Juice pulled alongside Mama and pulled a glum face.

'Looks like it's gonna be a pretty lousy trip,' he observed moodily.

Mama smiled grimly back at him, and nodded.

The Angels cruised into the town and headed for the main square. Mama led them round the clock-tower twice and up the road behind the bus station. She wheeled into a huge summer car park which was virtually deserted and parked the Harley.

'Well - it looks as though the fuzz have this town pretty well uptight,' she announced to her morose followers. 'Guess we'll just have to behave ourselves.'

They dismounted slowly, uncertain of what to do.

'We'll take a walk through town,' said Mama. '...And remember, if anyone has to get out in a hurry - it's straight back to the clubhouse with no stopping.'

The Angels nodded miserably in understanding. Mama swaggered away from the bikes and led them towards the square again. She turned into the Gardens.

The path which led through the lawn and beautifully-kept flowerbeds of the Gardens was wide, and edged with a small but clearly marked wire border. 'Keep Of the Grass' signs were much in evidence.

Mama glanced down at them and smiled. The sign which applied to Hells Angels had yet to be invented. Stepping slowly and deliberately across the border, she led her troop across the lush grass.

The ground, sodden with recent rain, sank beneath the weight of booted feet. The perfect lawn, one of Bournemouth's pride and joys, soon bore the ugly scars of footsteps and the scuffing of heels.

Mama glanced behind her, looking for lurking fuzz or prowling park-keepers. Seeing none, she hurriedly crossed to a nearby flower-bed and pulled up a thin bamboo stake which had been supporting a small bush. Wielding the stick like a rapier, she slashed the tops off daffodils and budding tulips with sadistic pleasure.

Her followers soon followed her example. They progressed through the gardens, leaving a trail of senseless destruction and vandalism in their wake.

Soapy produced a Webley air pistol from his belt and began to shoot at feeding birds. Having no success, he turned his attention to shooting at the coloured bulbs which adorned the night-time illuminations. These static targets were more susceptible to his erratic marksmanship. He smashed two or three dozen before he tired of the game and returned the gun to his belt.

The mob reached the end of the lawns and stepped back on to the path which led out to the sea-front.

A few people walked about, taking the sea air and a little exercise. The sky had become overcast since leaving London, and it was threatening rain. The lack of an audience increased the Angels' sense of boredom and frustration.

Soapy whipped out his pistol again and fired half a dozen slugs at a line of seagulls, sitting on a decorated lamp standard. Freaky stepped forward with a sneer and snatched the pistol from his grasp.

'You couldn't hit a bloody barn,' he jeered, holding out his palm for a supply of pellets. Grudgingly, Soapy fished in his pockets and tipped half a dozen slugs into his hand.

'Right,' said Freaky, loading the pistol and taking careful aim. 'You gotta allow for these things to jump...aim low.'

He rested the pistol across his crooked left arm, using it as a support.

The air pistol hissed, and a seagull rose into the air with a flurry of wings and a cry of pain. Protected by its heavy matting of down feathers it flew away unscathed.

'You gotta hit 'em in the right place,' Freaky explained rather sheepishly. He reloaded and fired off another shot which missed.

Three shots later, he scored a direct hit. With a shriek of pain, a seagull fluttered to the ground to fall upon the pavement with a heavy thud. It lay there injured, its wings beating feebly as it tried to escape into the air once again.

Freaky fell upon the injured bird with a shriek of joy. He picked it up by the neck, curling his other hand carefully around its body to stop the wings from flapping.

'Put a slug through its head, Freak...put it out of its misery,' suggested Danny the Deathlover. Freaky looked down at his booty reflectively.

'Tell you what,' he said finally, with a flash of inspiration. 'I got a better idea...I reckon we ought to pluck this damn bird while it's still alive...that'd be really a mind-snapper.'

He looked all around for a suitable audience. 'Mind-snappers' were of little function except to horrify or antagonise citizens.

His eyes fell upon a couple of old-age pensioners sitting quietly on a nearby bench. Grinning, he walked towards them, clutching the still-struggling bird in his arms.

He walked in front of the bench and stood only a few feet from the elderly couple. They glanced up at him quizzically, seeing the injured bird cradled in his arms.

'Oh, the poor thing,' said the old lady, deeply touched. 'Is it injured?'

'Yeah...sort of,' said Freaky, grinning widely. The old dear had obviously assumed that he was an animal lover.

Slowly, deliberately, he reached out his fingers and grasped a thick bunch of feathers between his finger and thumb. Wrenching them out, he lifted his hand into the air and let the plucked feathers flutter to the ground.

While the old couple looked on in shocked horror, he repeated the procedure and laughed wickedly. 'We're gonna eat it when it's ready,' he informed them in a serious voice. He plucked out another bunch of feathers and threw them towards the bench.

The agonised bird struggled feverishly in his arms.

The old lady scrambled to her feet and advanced on Freaky slowly.

'You disgusting...animal,' she hissed with deep loathing in her voice. 'You're savages, the lot of you...you're not fit to share this earth with decent folk.'

Freaky ducked backwards and laughed in her face. This was exactly the reaction he loved. It was, as he had imagined, a real mind-snapper.

He tore out more feathers and danced forward to throw them in the woman's face like a shower of white petals.

'That's enough, Freaky,' snapped Danny suddenly. He jumped forward to prize the tortured seagull from Freaky's clutches. Throwing the bird to the pavement heavily, he stamped hard upon its head. Satisfied the creature was dead and beyond pain, he turned abruptly on his heels and walked away.

'Hey, Man...I didn't know you was an animal lover,' Freaky taunted him. Danny whirled suddenly, his face livid with anger.

'I like some animals a frigging sight more than I like some people,' Danny screamed at him. 'You coulda just killed it.'

'Christ, Man...don't get uptight,' blustered Freaky, ducking away. 'It was just for a laugh, that's all.'

Danny moved as if to throw a punch, then seemed to change his mind. He turned on his heel abruptly.

'Forget it,' he snapped wearily. He looked shamefaced at the others and tried to grin. It didn't quite come off. He was embarrassed at having shown emotion in front of them.

Somehow it lacked class.

A few of the Angels laughed nervously and tried to forget the incident.

'Let's go take a look at the beach,' suggested Dirty Dick. They headed for the promenade blindly, thankful for a lead.

The tide was fully in. The Angels stared at the sea moodily for a few seconds and walked away again.

'This town's a shithole,' muttered Mama disgustedly. 'Let's get the hell out.'

Miserably her followers turned to walk back through the gardens to the hogs.

'There they are,' screamed a voice a little distance away. Mama looked along the path to where a frantic park official was talking to three coppers. They stood by the ravaged flowerbeds...and now the keeper was pointing directly at them.

Mama looked at the three cops and thought quickly. Under normal circumstances there would be no point in running - but perhaps she could use the situation to her own advantage.

As the three constables started to run towards them, Mama made up her mind quickly. This was her chance to get rid of the main bunch.

'We'd better scatter,' she called out. 'No point in hanging around and asking for bother.'

She turned quickly to her right, where Juice and Julie stood.

'Don't forget,' she hissed. 'Back at the cafe.'

Juice winked at her briefly and peeled away to make his break. Mama stood her ground for a while until the police were only fifty yards away. Ethel had moved up to stand by her side and Danny the Deathlover waited patiently for the move.

'OK...run for it,' shouted Mama and jumped on to the grass. She streaked away across the lawn at a tangent from the approaching law, heading straight for an ornamental flowerbed and rockery.

'They won't want to put their flat feet through that lot,' she shouted behind her as she ran. 'They don't like to damage the greenery.'

She was right. The cops stopped, looked at Mama's fleeing party and then back to the other scattering groups. They chose to pursue a group of Angels who were running back towards the sea front.

Mama dived right through the flower beds, her flying feet destroying blooms and shrubs like a runaway scythe. Jumping over an ornamental pond, she started to scramble up the rockery.

Ethel and Danny followed her closely. Danny had made up his mind to stick close to her no matter what. He wanted to see what plans were afoot, and deter mama from any stupid moves if he could.

At the top of the rockery, a clump of pine trees gave them adequate cover. Mama stopped behind a thick trunk to regain her breath.

The three fugitives looked back down over the gardens. Two of the coppers had managed to grab an Angel each, but from this distance, it was impossible to identify them. The third cop was still running round in small circles, threatening to disappear up his own blue arsehole at any second.

Mama pointed up through the pine trees towards a main road which ran alongside the edge of the gardens.

'That's Westover Road,' she said. 'It loops round the square.'

'How we gonna get back to the hogs?' Ethel demanded. 'The fuzz will be straight up there to intercept us.'

'No - they won't bother,' said Mama confidently. 'They got bigger problems than a few bloody flowers.'

'I dunno so much,' muttered Danny. 'I heard before they're pretty tough down here on vandalism. I reckon we ought to wait a while before we go back.'

Mama looked up at the Westover Road and grinned.

'Nope...I got a much better idea,' she said. 'I know this town inside out...we're gonna take a bus.'

She broke away and ran up towards the road.

Danny and Ethel exchanged a brief look for puzzlement and followed her.

Mama vaulted a low metal railing which separated the gardens from the road and waited for the other two to join her.

'There she is,' she cried, pointing to the front of a green bus standing at a nearby stop. On the indicator board, the words 'Bus Depot' were written clearly.

She ran towards it, jumping on to the platform just as the bus began to move away. Danny and Ethel just made it behind her.

They ran up the stairs, ignoring the curses and shouts from the conductor.

He came racing up the stairs after them.

'Are you bloody deaf?' he wanted to know. 'We're not carrying any passengers. This bus is just going back to the depot.'

'Yeah - we know,' said Mama coolly. 'That's where we wanna go.'

The conductor looked at her evilly for a second, and his hand strayed towards the bell.

He glanced out of the window. They were almost at the bus station anyway. He shrugged his shoulders resignedly and retreated back down the stairs.

As the bus trundled into the station, Mama led the way down the stairs to stand on the platform. She looked out over the car park where the hogs were stored. A solitary Panda car had just made its appearance, and was cruising along the line of bikes.

A few Angels appeared at the bottom of the car park and the Panda car quickly turned to give chase.

Mama laughed gleefully.

'Here's our chance,' she said. 'Run for it.'

They jumped off the still-moving bus and started running as soon as their feet touched the ground.

They were astride the hogs before the fuzz noticed them, but by that time it was too late. A Morris Minor was no match for three fast motorbikes.

They streaked out of the car park, down the street towards the clock in the square and raced round the perimeter of the traffic roundabout.

Peeling off, Mama revved the engine hard and shot up the steep hill which led to Boscombe. Pedestrians and other road-users stared at them in fascination as they accelerated into the sixties and kept right on moving.

Mama continued to drive recklessly for several miles. Finally she slowed down to a comfortable cruising speed and turned to grin at Ethel and Danny.

'Well, that was a pretty lousy afternoon, wasn't it?' she asked with a laugh.

Ethel grinned back at her good-naturedly.

'Well it keeps us off the streets, don't it?' he observed wryly.

CHAPTER THIRTEEN

REHEARSAL

They sat in the transport cafe over cups of long-cold tea and waited. Mama's hands fidgeted constantly, the incessant flickering of her eyes betraying her nervousness and impatience.

'Reckon the fuzz got 'em?' asked Ethel finally.

'Don't be bloody daft,' Mama snapped at him - but her voice lacked total conviction. 'Juice is too smart for those dumb bastards,' she added, as if to convince herself. 'They'll be along soon.'

They continued to wait, as the evening wore on, and the clientele of the cafe changed constantly.

'Exactly what you got cooking?' asked Danny the Deathlover at last.

Mama smiled her secretive smile at him.

'I'm not really sure...yet,' she said. 'But something's bound to occur to me.'

She stood up, pushing her chair back from the table with a squeal.

'I can't just sit here,' she muttered irritably. 'I'm going out for a ride and look round.'

The tone of her voice precluded either Danny or Ethel rising to join her. Mama wanted to be on her own.

She walked out of the cafe towards the hogs, and roared off down the road.

Danny and Ethel sat silently for a few seconds.

'What's she planning, Ethel?' asked Danny at length.

Ethel shrugged his shoulders.

'Dunno,' he said grinning. 'But whatever it is, I reckon she'll make it exciting. At least we're never short for kicks when Mama's got a bee in her bonnet.'

'But it ain't being Angels, is it?' Danny pointed out quietly.

Ethel pursed his lips reflectively.

'No, I suppose it ain't,' he agreed finally. 'But what the hell?'

Danny turned away in disgust, and sat staring into his teacup moodily. If only he knew what Mama was planning, perhaps he would find a way to fight it. As it was, he was on his own, knowing nothing, and unable to make a single constructive move.

The roar of motorbikes made him look up towards the door. The noise of the engines stopped, and Juice, Julie and three of his riders swaggered into the cafe. They saw Danny and Ethel sitting at the table, and a frown crossed Juice's face as he realised Mama was absent.

'Where's Mama?' he asked quickly. 'She didn't get caught, did she?'

Ethel smiled. 'No - she's just gone for a little run,' he explained. 'Anyway...what held you up for so long?'

Juice grinned widely. 'Them bloody fuzz was swarming all round the hogs like fruit flies time we got to 'em,' he said. 'A few of the boys got pulled, so we waited it out until they got fed up and went to arrest a few drunks. Then we grabbed the hogs and came straight here. Superspade and Freaky are just behind us.'

As if to corroborate his words, the black grinning face of Superspade appeared in the door. He strolled in, closely followed by Freaky.

They sat down at the table while Juice sent Julie up to the serving counter to get teas for them all.

She returned with a laden tray and they sipped reflectively, awaiting Mama's return.

A half hour passed. Outside, it had grown dark, and the cafe began to fill up with lorry drivers who had pulled off the road for supper.

A blast of motorcycle horns made them start suddenly.

'Who the hell's that?' asked Juice, scrambling to his feet quickly. 'That sounds like my horn.' He ran out of the cafe, hotly pursued by two of his boys.

The rest waited patiently for a few minutes. When Juice reappeared, he was grinning all over his face, and there was a devilish gleam in his cold eyes.

'It was Mama,' he whispered softly as he sat down. 'She didn't want to come back in here...it looks like we're about to see some action.'

Ethel clambered to his feet.

'Come on then - let's ride,' he said.

Juice reached out to grab him by the sleeve and pull him back down to his chair.

'Be cool,' he hissed. 'Mama said not to attract too much attention.'

He turned to Julie.

'Give us the goodies, luv,' he whispered.

She shrugged, fumbled in her handbag and produced the hypodermic syringe case. She passed it to him under cover of the table.

'Won't be a minute,' he muttered, standing up and walking in the direction of the gent's toilet. When he re-emerged, a moment later, there was a strange spring in his step and an even wilder gleam in his eyes.

'Wowee...now I'm ready for anything,' he said exultantly as he handed the hypo furtively back to Julie. 'Come on...let's get going...only finish your drinks and make like we're blowing for good.'

The Angels obediently slurped down the remainder of their teas and rose to their feet noisily.

'Time to hit the road,' said Juice loudly, making sure the other occupants of the cafe heard him clearly.

They filed out of the transport cafe and crossed the dimly-lit forecourt. Mama waited for them in the shadows, stepping out to greet them as they approached.

Her followers, with the exception of the grinning Juice, looked at her in utter amazement. She was a completely different person.

The leather suit, the helmet and her originals had been discarded, revealing the thin sweater and faded blue jeans she had been wearing underneath. Her long blonde hair was piled up and hidden under a curly black wig, and her face was plastered with heavy vivid make-up.

She cut short the barrage of questions with a wave of her hand.

'Now listen,' she snapped quickly. 'I want you all to follow Juice up the road to the first cross-roads...he'll explain everything when you get there. Ethel...you stay with me.'

'Let's go,' muttered Juice, and led the way to the hogs. The puzzled Angels followed him blindly, leaving an equally mystified Ethel behind them.

'Now, since I left the caff, everyone's changed around a

bit...right?' Mama asked.

Ethel nodded dumbly.

'...So no one in there at the moment has seen me before...OK?'

Again, Ethel could only nod his affirmation.

Mama smiled cunningly.

'D'ya reckon I'd make a good pick-up for a quick screw?' she asked him suddenly.

Ethel stared at her blankly.

'I mean, would you pick me up as a hitch-hiker...if you was a randy lorry driver?' Mama went on.

'Yeah - I suppose so,' answered Ethel in a puzzled voice.

'Right then...we're in business,' said Mama gleefully. 'Now here's what I want you to do.' She pointed across the cafe forecourt and down the road.

'See that little lay-by there?' she asked. Ethel looked, and nodded his head.

'OK...now you take your hog and wait down there...only don't take your eyes off me for a second,' Mama went on. 'I'm going to get myself picked up by a lorry driver...and as soon as you see me actually get into the cab, you belt right down that road for about half a mile until you meet up with the others. Juice will fill you in from there.'

'OK,' grunted Ethel. 'I don't know what the hell is going on...but it sounds like a giggle.' He winked at her before walking across to his hog. 'Best of luck,' he whispered.

Mama smiled back at him, turned and walked back to the cafe.

She wiggled in through the door sexily, and made her way to the counter. Several pairs of eyes followed her greedily as she propped herself up against it, and turned to face the clientele. She stood there suggestively, with her hand on one hip and her full breasts pushed out proudly.

She ordered a cup of tea, and wiggled across the cafe once again, making sure that every man in the place had taken a good look at the merchandise. She sat, sipped at her tea reflectively and eyed up a group of drivers who sat at a nearby table.

They returned her wandering eye enthusiastically, with

much nudging each other and whispered remarks. One of the drivers leant forwards across the table to mutter something to his colleagues and they laughed dirtily.

The bait was laid. The fish was half-hooked. Mama rose from her seat and slithered over to her admirers.

'Any of you boys going Southampton way?' she asked bluntly.

Two of the lorry drivers raised their eyebrows expressively.

'Might be,' said one of them suggestively. 'Depends, don't it?'

'Thought one of you might like a bit of company,' Mama said quietly. 'Wanna get down to the docks, don't I?'

'Got some....business down at the docks, have you?' asked one of the drivers and leered smuttily. The inference was plain, and Mama played him along beautifully.

'What do you think?' she asked, and wriggled her torso sensuously. 'Well...anyone gonna give us a ride?'

'Ride for a ride, eh?' asked one of the men, becoming bolder.

Mama flashed him a fiery look.

'Why not?' she said. 'One good turn deserves another, don't it?'

The two drivers who had first spoken to her exchanged rapid glances. It was obvious they both fancied the opportunity...but which of them would get the prize?

'Go on, Bert...you take her,' said the younger one after a moment's pause. 'I get my share anyway...reckon you could use a bit of relaxation.' He nudged his colleague and leered at the others. The older lorry driver licked his lips, and a dreamy smile spread across his face.

'OK lover,' he said slowly. 'I'll give you a ride. Just hang on for a few minutes until I've finished me tea.'

He turned to his cup and swilled it down hurriedly.

'OK, let's go,' he said abruptly, rising to his feet.

Mama followed him meekly out of the cafe and across the forecourt to where the lorries were parked. The driver fished in his pockets and carefully unlocked the driver's door of the cab. As he stepped in, he sorted out another key from his bundle and inserted it into a small box built into the floor.

'Theft alarm,' he explained, climbing up into the cab. He reached across to open the other door.

'Hop in then love,' he said, putting the ignition key in the lock.

Mama hopped in beside him, slamming the door. She smiled inwardly as she heard the muffled growl of Ethel's hog streaking up the road.

The driver's fingers dropped from the ignition lock slowly. He half-turned in the darkened cab to face her.

'How's about a little bit on account,' he leered, straining towards her.

'Not here...people will see,' hissed Mama, drawing away tauntingly. 'Out on the road...eh?'

'OK,' snapped the driver wearily, sitting up straight in his seat. 'But you'd better not be conning me...you know?'

Mama smiled sexily.

'Don't worry pops...you'll get your jollies,' she murmured with a sexy chuckle.

She sat back as the huge lorry rumbled out of the car park and on to the road.

They ground slowly down the road. The lorry was obviously carrying a heavy load. Mama kept her eyes peeled, staring through the windscreen, noting the road illuminated in the carpet of light from the lorry's head lamps and straining to see into the pitch blackness beyond.

A full minute passed slowly. Mama felt the tension of excitement building up inside.

She saw the flash of headlights a split second before she heard the driver's muffled curse.

'What the Hell...?' he muttered in a puzzled voice as his foot moved to hover over the brake pedal.

A solid line of blazing headlights blocked the road. The lorry slowed with a hiss of air from the brakes and crept to a complete halt. Even with the lorry's headlights on full beam, it was practically impossible to see anything except the blinding dazzle of the hog head lamps. The riders could be picked out, but their faces were just blurred white blobs.

The lorry driver reached for the door handle and swung open the cab door. He stepped out warily, wondering just

111

what was happening.

Mama reached over suddenly and delivered a quick rabbit-punch on the back of his neck. He slumped forwards, half-stepping and half-falling out of the driving cab down to the road. From the side of the lorry, Ethel stepped forwards quickly and clubbed him over the head with a tyre lever before he could pick himself up. Dragging the unconscious man on to the grass verge by the side of the road, he speedily ran back, climbed up into the cab and slammed the lorry into gear. He eased it a few yards further up the road and turned the corner by the crossroads.

He switched off the ignition, and his eyes searched the dashboard until he found the light switch. He flipped it up, extinguishing the lorry's headlights.

Mama opened the door and jumped down from the high cab. She landed on her toes, sprang round and called to the waiting Angels.

'OK fellers...come here, quick.'

They gathered round her, surprised by the speed of the operation and wondering vaguely what to do next.

Juice had already started to unhitch the tailboard of the lorry. He peered inside with the aid of a flashlight.

'Christ...there's only bloody great crates of machinery,' he complained. 'What the hell are we going to do with this lot?'

'Forget it,' called Mama, already walking away from the lorry towards her hog. 'We ain't gonna touch it...nothing there of any use, anyway.'

She climbed astride the Harley and kicked it alive. Juice ran from the back of the lorry to her side. His face was puzzled.

'What was the point of all that, then?' he asked. 'If we wasn't gonna pinch the load?'

Mama smiled as she reached up to take off the wig.

'That was just a dress rehearsal,' she explained. 'Sort of like a try-out to get you guys into practice. We're gonna pull just one job like that...exactly like that...only it's gonna be the really big one...and we'll know before we pull it exactly what load it's carrying.'

She busied herself stepping back into her leather costume which was tucked away underneath the saddle. She slipped on the helmet, snapped on the straps and revved up her hog.

'Come on...don't hang about,' she snapped, slipping the bike into gear. 'Let's get back to London, fast.'

As she spoke, the glare of approaching headlights appeared further up the road.

The Angels need no second bidding. Quickly rousing their hogs into screaming life, they streaked off down the road, leaving their 'rehearsal' victim to regain consciousness or be discovered by a passer-by.

What mattered was that the heist had been proved feasible. All that was needed now was the perfect target.

CHAPTER FOURTEEN

THE CRUNCH

For the next two weeks, the Angels saw little of Mama. She was entirely dedicated to her project. Day and night she was out, touring the motorways and the trunk roads, stopping in every transport cafe, sizing each one for peak times, slack times and ease of getaway.

In her absence, Danny the Deathlover filled in his own time and the needs of the Hells Angels by assuming a tighter command. He organised small runs, kept the committee informed of the normal Angel activities and made sure that subs were paid into the treasury. When rumours were abroad about the 'something big' that Mama was planning, Danny quashed them or invented plausible cover stories.

Now, more than ever before, he sensed powers of leadership in himself that he had long feared to recognise. If he had not been so pre-occupied and worried with Elaine and her crazy plans, it would have been an enjoyable time for him.

Juice James let Danny have his head, conscious of the fact that Danny was closer to the true spirit of the Angels then he felt himself. Like Mama, he had become obsessed with the American Dream, living from day to day in a half-world created by his fantasies and his drug habit.

The rest of the Angels who were fully in the know also lived through a strange fortnight - oddly detached from reality by the sense of tension and excitement which gripped them. It was as if the one single factor which would change their lives radically was almost, but not quite, pushed in front of them. The plan had been outlined, all but for this final detail. It was definite...yet not yet quite real until the actual time came. They were mentally committed to the act, but could still preserve a vestige of free choice. Perhaps, when the time came, they could still duck out, refuse to go through with it.

They waited expectantly, content to pass away the time by continuing to be Hells Angels.

At last, the reality came. Mama had found the ideal hit.

'Cigarettes,' she told Juice and his boys excitedly. 'Fifty thousand quid's worth of cigarettes. Every Friday the same driver takes the load from Bristol up to the London depot for distribution. He stops at a caff just outside Reading for a bite to eat somewhere between nine and ten.'

Juice whistled between his teeth.

'Jeezus! Fifty thousand,' he repeated in awe. 'Ain't that too big, Mama?'

'No...it's right...the whole frigging thing is right...listen, Man, fags are the ideal haul...they're fast to turn over, high-profit stuff and about the best price and weight relationship you could hope for. I've checked with a couple of villains in the East End...they'll take the lot for ten thousand cash.'

'But you said there was fifty thousand quid's worth,' muttered Juice dumbly. 'What happened to the other forty grand?'

'Christ, Juice, you don't expect to get the bloody price on the packet from a fence, you dumb bastard.' Mama swore at him irritably. 'They gotta make some bread out of it too, you know.'

Juice pondered on this point for a second.

'Seems a bloody con to me,' he mumbled shirtily. 'Bloody load of crooks.'

The humour of his last remark seemed to escape him. Mama ignored it and carried on outlining the plan.

'The caff is just right...there's a small side road about two miles up the road...that's where we'll hit,' she went on. 'The only trouble is that it'll be too light to follow the pattern of the rehearsal...so I'm gonna have to make a few changes in the basic plan.'

'Like what?' Superspade wanted to know.

'Well, there's gonna be too much traffic on the main road to pull it there,' Mama told him. 'So I'm gonna have to persuade him to pull off the main drag into this side road. That's where you'll be waiting. Ethel drives the lorry back here to the clubhouse, you get here ahead of him and unload the stuff fast. Then Ethel dumps the lorry out on the South Circular somewhere, and the fuzz automatically assume it's an East End mob.'

'How the hell are you gonna persuade the guy to pull off the road?' asked Ethel. 'He ain't going to take much notice of a woman, is he?'

'I've thought of that,' answered Mama coldly. 'And that's one of the little changes...I'm gonna have to take along a little persuader.'

'Like what?' Ethel asked.

Mama grinned mysteriously, and crossed the clubhouse to the locked armoury trunk.

Unlocking it, she pulled out a bundle of old rags and carried it over to them again. She unwrapped it carefully, finally cradling the contents almost lovingly in her arms.

Juice's eyes nearly popped out of their sockets as he saw it. A sawn-off twelve-bore shotgun!

'Christ - you ain't gonna use a friggin gun,' cried Ethel in alarm. 'Hell, Mama, I reckon on robbery, but I'm screwed if I'm gonna go for murder. Man, that's too much of a trip for me.'

'I ain't gonna murder anyone,' Mama sneered at him. 'I don't have to fire it, do I? It's just a sure-fire guarantee that the guy is going to do what he's told - with this thing poking in his ribs.'

'Where the hell did you get that?' was all Juice wanted to know.

'Picked it up from the same villains who're gonna take the stuff,' said Mama. 'Cost me eighty quid...but it's going to be an investment, ain't it?'

Danny the Deathlover had been sitting quietly for long enough. Things were rapidly becoming even worse than he had feared.

He stood up, snatched the shotgun from Mama's hands and laid it gently on the floor. He stood above her, arms crossed and a look of defiance flashing in his eyes.

'For Christ's sake come back to Earth, Mama,' he pleaded. 'You can't pull a job like this...Good God Almighty...this is big league stuff. Let's kick this stupid game in the head, shall we?'

Elaine looked at him in amazement.

'You think this is a bloody game?' she screamed after a slight pause. 'Is it too much for you, kiddo? Wanna go and play Speedway stars instead, do you?'

'Mama...you can't do it,' repeated Danny in a hopeless, pleading voice. 'For God's sake...can't you see sense?'

Mama stared at him with undisguised contempt for a few seconds more, then turned her back on him abruptly.

'All right,' she screamed. 'Any more of you brave boys want to duck out?'

She stared at each face in turn. Several pairs of eyes met hers, shifted uneasily and flickered away again. Half a minute passed in stunned, awkward silence.

Superspade clambered to his feet.

'Call me chicken if you like,' he muttered. 'But I ain't going for any shooting...and as long as you got that gun, you might just use it.' He shuffled awkwardly on his feet, and started to move backwards slowly. 'No, Mama...I'm out of this one.'

He turned slowly, and walked towards the door.

Mama didn't bother to shout anything after him. She knew that Superspade had all the guts in the world where it counted. This just wasn't his scene, that was all.

'Anyone else?' she questioned again.

Freaky opened his mouth to speak, but only a frightened stammer came out.

'It's too big,' he managed to blurt out at last. 'It's too risky.'

Max the Knife and Pee Wee rose with him, nodding their heads in dumb agreement. They backed away sheepishly.

Mama looked again at everyone in the room. Her eyes met Juice's and flashed the unspoken question.

'We said we'd do it...so we'll do it,' he whispered softly.

Mama turned her attention to his three companions. Soapy, Dirty Dick and Little Ed exchanged glances between themselves, and finally looked back at her.

'OK...we're in,' muttered Little Ed, speaking for all of them.

'Grass...Trucker...Ethel?' snapped Mama.

'We're with you,' said Ethel with a grim smile.

'That's eight then,' said Mama quietly. 'That's enough...So the job's on - this Friday.'

'Looks that way,' put in Juice, with a nervous laugh.

Mama turned to Danny, who still sat there.

'You might as well fuck off, Danny,' she said quietly. 'The Hells Angels need you to play scoutmaster.'

Danny stared at her levelly, and spoke in calmer tones. He had been thinking rapidly during the last few minutes, and had realised that he must have a chance of stopping the crazy venture as long as he stayed around.

'No...I'm in with you,' he lied. 'Nobody can ever say I'm chicken.'

Mama stared at him questioningly for a moment, then a smile broke across her face.

'Good,' she said happily. 'You'll like America, Danny.'

She turned to the others.

'OK...we meet here at seven o'clock on Friday,' she said firmly.

Mama started to walk out.

'Just one thing,' Ethel called after her. 'How can you be so sure this driver is going to offer you a ride?'

Mama turned slowly to face him, a devilish grin on her face. Her fingers reached up to grasp the catch on her zipper.

With one sudden, smooth movement, she slashed open her costume to the waist, exposing the whiteness of her body against the dull sheen of the black leather. Her ripe breasts spilled out and jiggled gently.

'Wouldn't you?' she asked him pointedly.

Ethel didn't bother to answer. Mama pulled the zipper up again, turned and walked out.

CHAPTER FIFTEEN

THE RAID

They were all tooled up and ready to go...everyone with the exception of Juice and Julie.

Mama paced the floor of the clubroom impatiently, glancing at her watch every half minute.

At twenty past seven, Juice staggered into the clubhouse, and Mama knew something was wrong at once.

His face was a dirty shade of grey, like fine cigar ash, and his mouth was contorted with pain. He hurried towards her, and stood there shaking and trembling as though with St Vitus' dance. His left arm dangled limply by his side.

'What's up, Man?' asked Mama with concern.

Juice gritted his teeth, and tried to force a brave smile on to his face.

'Looks like I'm going to have to miss the big one,' he hissed angrily, pointing to the injured arm.

With his right hand, he picked carefully at the material of his left sleeve, rolling it up gently. Just below the elbow, an ugly black and yellow bruise started to show. Juice finished rolling up the sleeve as far as his bicep, and Mama looked aghast at the huge swelling on his upper arm. It was easily twice its normal size, and from the centre of the swelling, an open sore was discharging an unsightly mixture of blood and thick yellow pus.

It was obvious that the arm was completely useless.

'Bloody festered, ain't it?' grunted Juice. 'Must have been a dirty needle.'

Ethel looked over Mama's shoulder, saw the arm and shuddered with distaste.

'Looks like we're gonna have to cancel everything,' he muttered sadly.

Mama looked briefly at the crestfallen Juice, then at Ethel and the others.

'No,' she stated flatly. 'We're not going to cancel now. We're going ahead as planned...we'll just be one man short, that's all. Anyway - the plan isn't critical...we can do the job with eight quite easily.'

'I don't know,' Ethel muttered nervously. 'I reckon it's an omen.'

Mama looked at him in amazement, finally breaking into a laugh.

'Christ, I didn't know you were superstitious,' she said.

Ethel shuffled his feet awkwardly.

'I ain't,' he blustered. 'But I reckon there are bad luck signs.'

'Don't talk stupid,' snapped Mama angrily. 'There ain't nothing gonna go wrong.'

She turned to Juice and smiled in apology.

'Sorry, Man,' she said.

Juice forced a smile.

'Sorry I let you down, Mama,' he said. 'But best of luck, anyway...I'll be waiting for you when you get back.'

'Yeah. See you then,' muttered Elaine, slapping him gently on the back. She led her small band of followers out of the clubhouse without looking back.

Outside, she paused briefly before mounting her hog to check everything. She wore her 'civvies' already, and her black leather costume, the wig and the shotgun were carefully packed into a black duffel bag which she slung over her shoulder.

Satisfied that she had everything she needed, she mounted the Harley and roared off at breakneck pace. It was important that they made up for the lost time.

It was eight-thirty when they roared past the small transport cafe on the A4. Mama led them up the main road for about a mile and a half until they came to the crossroads.

She stopped, and pointed down the quiet side-road.

'You all wait here,' she said, running her hog off the road and on to the grass verge.

She walked across to Soapy's hog and clambered across the pillion.

'OK Soapy...you get to be the lookout,' she snapped. 'Back to the cafe.'

She turned to her followers for one last quick run-through of the plan. They understood it perfectly. Mama fished in the duffel bag, pulled out the wig and deftly slipped it on. She tucked her helmet to the bottom of the bag and lifted out the shotgun for a last check. There were two cartridges in the breech...useful for making a convincing noise if the situation warranted. Satisfied, she tucked the gun carefully down the side of the bag and covered the butt with a yellow scarf.

'OK Soapy - let's go,' she said, waving to the others as they roared back towards the cafe.

Soapy positioned himself behind a large advertising hoarding and watched Mama's retreating back as she walked into the cafe.

It was going to be a long, tense wait. He lit a cigarette and took long, nervous drags at it.

Once inside the cafe, Mama looked round and realised that she was only just in time. Her chosen victim had already finished his meal of hamburger and chips, and was swilling down the last of his tea.

He pushed back his seat and rose.

Elaine fumbled quickly with the duffel bag, making sure that the shotgun was well hidden. There was no other choice but to intercept him quickly.

She moved straight towards him, pushing her chest out and affecting a sexy wiggle.

'You going anywhere near London?' she asked brazenly. The lorry driver looked her over carefully, and a thoughtful look glazed his eyes.

'Yeah...so?' he questioned.

Mama was panicking slightly. There didn't seem to be enough time to go through the whole routine. She decided to crash it into one hit or miss effort.

'I'd make it well worth your while if you'd give me a ride,' she muttered sexily. 'I've got to get into town by ten o'clock. I'll do anything...anything at all.'

The driver looked her over from head to toe without shame or embarrassment. His eyes feasted on the smooth mounds of her breasts and the swell of her hips.

'OK,' he said curtly, as though doing her a very personal favour. 'I'll buy it.'

Mama fluttered her eyelashes at him sexily.

'Thank you,' she said. Then, with a coy smile: 'You won't regret it.'

The driver laughed coarsely.

'You're damned right I won't,' he said. 'You're going to deliver the goodies before we leave here.' He turned away from her to shout across the cafe to the man serving behind the counter.

121

'Here, Joe,' he shouted. 'OK if I use the back room for ten minutes?' He jerked his thumb towards Elaine and winked suggestively. The owner held up his hand with one thumb held upwards.

The driver turned his attention back to Mama.

'OK, then?' he shot at her. 'Joe's a buddy of mine...we can use the bedroom out back.'

Elaine panicked. She hadn't allowed for anything like this.

'Can't we sort of get to know each other a little bit first?' she blustered, trying to look sexy and promising yet anxious to stall him.

'OK lovie...you want to forget it, we'll forget it,' said the lorry driver casually. 'I've been conned by you little prick-teasers before...I know your game. All bloody promises and then screams of rape when you've got your lift. Well not me, darling...I'm too old in the tooth to fall for that one anymore.'

He turned to walk off. Mama clutched at his sleeve anxiously.

'No...wait,' she cried. 'I wouldn't con you...honest. I really have got to get to London...we'll do like you say.'

'That's better,' grunted the driver, grabbing her by the elbow and propelling her towards the door at the back of the cafe.

They walked through, followed by a chorus of lewd remarks and dirty laughs from the other drivers.

Blindly, her mind reeling, Elaine let herself be pushed into the small, dirty bedroom. It wasn't really a bedroom, just a small spare room with no furniture except an old divan bed with a torn, soiled mattress on top. Joe must keep it especially for this purpose, Mama thought as her companion thrust her roughly towards the bed.

'OK love...get your bloody drawers off,' he said bluntly, fumbling with the belt on his trousers.

He stripped off his pants, and walked slowly towards her. There was no attempt at seduction, no sweet words of tenderness. This was a business transaction, pure and simple.

Mama tried to ignore the reek of his sweaty body as he lowered himself on top of her...

Outside Soapy looked at his watch for the twentieth time and lit another cigarette. He wondered what was taking so long.

At the crossroads, Danny the Deathlover was thinking fast,

and analysing his chances of stopping the operation even at this late stage. The fact the Juice was absent was in his favour, he thought. Danny was well enough respected throughout the Angels to be listened to.

'Look...it ain't too late to call this bloody thing off,' he said to Ethel. 'We can belt back down to the caff before Mama leaves and tell her we ain't gonna go through with it.'

'Now why should we do a thing like that?' asked Ethel, eyeing him coldly. 'You getting cold feet again?'

Danny gestured around him to the others, who stood fidgeting nervously.

'Isn't everybody?' he asked. 'Don't you think that we're all biting off too much?'

He turned away from Ethel, directing his remarks at the main bunch.

'How about it fellers...how about cutting the scene altogether?'

A low murmur of conversation rippled round, and in that split second Danny realised for the first time that none of them really wanted to go through with it. They had been carried away by the excitement...dragged this far by the sheer devilment...and now all that stopped them backing out was a sense of stubborn pride. To back out now would show lack of class, brand them as chickens.

He seized on his sudden advantage, ignoring Ethel completely.

'Well...how about it?' he screamed at the top of his voice. 'Nobody can call us chicken just because be don't want to spend six bloody years in a jail cell...and for Christ's sake, that's the minimum we'll get for armed robbery.'

Danny wasn't even sure of the penalties they could incur, but six years sounded a frightening figure.

The Angels shifted on their feet even more uneasily.

'We're Hells Angels,' continued Danny. 'And that makes us rebels...but we don't have to prove how bloody rebellious we are by serving a prison stretch.'

He walked right up to Grass and Trucker.

'How about showing some REAL guts and splitting right now?' he pleaded with them. 'Let's just get on our hogs, get back down to that cafe and march in?'

Trucker flashed him an almost grateful look, then turned to Grass.

'Danny's talking sense, Man,' he muttered. 'How about it?'

Danny smiled triumphantly. The game was won and he knew it.

'Come on you mothers,' he screamed, racing across to his own hog. 'There may not be too much time.'

There was a fractional pause. Then, with an overwhelming sense of relief, they rushed after him.

Only Ethel stood his ground.

'You yellow bastards,' he called after them. 'Mama will rip your pretty little guts out for this.'

He stood there stubbornly, unable to move to follow them. With mixed feelings, he watched them zoom off down the road.

Danny raced down the road with his engine screaming. Recklessly, he swerved across the road and blasted through the cafe forecourt. Jumping off his hog, he kicked the footrest down hastily and left it with the engine ticking over. he ran into the cafe, pushing open the door.

The first glance told him Mama was not there. Bewildered, he backed out quickly, running back to his colleagues in alarm.

'She's already gone,' he shouted, his voice tinged with despair.

'What the hell's going on?'

Danny turned suddenly. It was Soapy, who had come out from behind his hiding place.

'When did Mama leave?' Danny asked abruptly.

Soapy looked at him stupidly.

'She ain't come out yet,' he answered. 'I been watching the door all the time.'

Danny forced his racing mind to concentrate, but nothing made sense. Bewildered, he could only stand there helplessly, unsure of what to do for the best.

At the rear of the cafe, Mama's erstwhile bedmate pushed open the back door and let Mama through. It was his first and only gentlemanly act of the evening.

'Lorry's out the back here,' he explained. 'Carrying a valuable load.'

A twinge of panic crossed Elaine's mind again. Suppose

Soapy didn't notice her in the lorry? She thought of the twin barrels of persuasion in her bag and felt slightly reassured. There was a certain degree of latitude within the plan.

She climbed into the cab and hitched the duffel bag on to her lap as the driver unlocked the various safety devices and started up the heavy truck.

She glanced nervously out of the windows for Soapy as the lorry rumbled round into the front car park.

For the first time, real fear and panic gripped her as she saw Danny and the Angels standing there. Instinctively, she started to reach for the door handle, but panic froze her.

A cold, hard knot of hate was also forming deep in her brain. Perhaps the great job would have to be called off, but the truck driver still had to pay for his brutal pleasure taken from her body. She remembered with loathing the feel of his dirty, smelly body upon hers and shivered with disgust and the desire for revenge.

Things had gone terribly wrong...and someone had to pay for it...

As the lorry gathered speed, her hands strayed towards the top of the duffel bag. Cautiously, her hand strayed inside and closed around the smooth butt of the shotgun.

She kept her eyes firmly fixed on the road ahead, looking out for the crossroads.

With a quarter of a mile to go, she slid the gun slowly out of the bag, curled her finger around the trigger and cradled it in her arms.

'My friend wants to stop,' she muttered icily.

The truck driver half-turned to her, saw the ugly double muzzle pointing at his belly and his face froze into a grim mask.

'Your friend usually get his way, does he,' he tried to joke, stalling for time. It could all be a preposterous hoax...some sort of sick joke.

Slowly, with an exaggerated movement, Elaine snapped off the safety catch.

The truck driver's face blanched as he realised with a sinking feeling that this was no joke.

He thought of his valuable load, thought of losing his job and thought of losing his life. Hell, there was no comparison.

'Where do you want me to stop?' he asked quietly.

'You're coming up to some crossroads,' Mama told him. 'Pull round to the left.'

The lorry driver nodded, sweat beginning to poor down his brow. He eased the lorry down through the gears and started to slow down...

'We'd better get back to the cross-roads,' said Danny at last. 'Maybe Mama left without Soapy noticing.' He ran to his hog and slewed it round in a tight circle in the car park. He was away down the road before the others had mounted their bikes...

The lorry ground to a halt.

'Open the door,' Mama snapped curtly. 'Then put you hands on your head and climb out.'

The driver did as he was told. He opened the cab door and started to ease himself out.

Mama turned the heavy shotgun in her hands, crashing the thick wooden butt into the back of his neck. He slumped across the seat. Manoeuvring herself round, Mama placed her boot in his back and pushed him roughly. He tumbled out into the road, where he lay in a crumpled heap.

Mama leapt out of the other side of the cab and shouted.

'Anyone there?'

Ethel came racing towards her.

'They chickened out,' he shouted. 'Danny talked the yellow bastards into chickening out.'

Mama glared at him with fury for a second.

'Fuck it, Man...we can do it ourselves,' she screamed. 'Go and hide your hog as best you can...only quickly.'

Ethel hesitated.

'They'll trace it,' he said. 'They'll be on to us in a matter of hours.'

'Jeezus, Ethel...with ten thousand in our pockets we can be out of the goddamn country in a few hours,' Mama shot at him. 'Hurry, Man...do what I say.'

Blindly, driven only by a sense of panic, Ethel obeyed.

Mama turned back to the lorry driver, who was beginning to recover.

She stepped over him quickly, hatred blazing in her eyes.

'I'm gonna make you pay for what you did to me,' she hissed.

'You filthy, dirty animal.'

She slammed the butt of the shotgun down into his ribs, hearing the rewarding crack of breaking bones.

She drew back her booted foot, slamming a vicious kick into his face. Another kick followed...and another, then another...

She drew back her leg once more.

With a superhuman effort, spurred on by fear and blinding pain, the lorry driver reached out, grasped her by the ankle and heaved.

Caught off balance, Mama tottered and fell.

The shotgun fell from her hands to fall with a clatter on the ground.

Desperately, the injured lorry driver reached out for it and scooped it up in his hands. Gritting his teeth against the pain which seared through his chest, he forced himself up on to his knees and levelled the gun at Elaine.

She faced it rigidly, frozen with fear like a cobra facing a mongoose. The driver's blood-streaked face was twisted with hatred and pain. His eyes were glassy, blank-looking.

Elaine saw death looking at her through two vacant eyes and her stomach turned to ice.

From behind, she heard the savage roar of a hog engine, and despite her fear, managed to throw a quick glance over her shoulder.

Danny the Deathlover bore down on the strange little tableau at full speed. He saw the two figures frozen in a still-life drama...saw the short, ugly shotgun pointed straight at Elaine's lovely face.

In a sudden, desperate decision, he ground back the throttle to seek the last ounce of power out of his Triumph. The machine responded eagerly, leaping forward to close the small gap.

Perhaps if he could smash the driver...enough to knock him aside, or smash the shotgun from his grasp.

Taken by surprise, the lorry driver looked up towards the sound of the approaching motorcycle and instinctively moved the shotgun towards this new danger.

Mama, seeing what she thought was a chance, dived for his waist, slamming a vicious punch into his groin at the same time.

The driver buckled with this extra pain, the last vestige of sanity left him and only the pain registered. His tortured body stiffened instinctively...and his finger squeezed back on the trigger, blasting off both barrels.

Danny the Deathlover caught the full blast at only a few feet range. His head and shoulders suddenly seemed to dissolve into a mangled, bloody pulp.

The hog, travelling at eighty miles an hour, continued as straight as a die on its course.

Elaine screamed as the world suddenly erupted into a flash of searing orange light and a wave of pain.

The maverick machine ploughed into the lorry driver, smashing his body against the side of the truck.

His mangled body poured out its life blood into the road, which mixed with Danny's in a dark pool.

Mama saw it all before she passed blissfully into unconsciousness.

CHAPTER SIXTEEN

EPILOGUE

Forty-two Hells Angels sat in the public gallery of the Central Criminal Court and stared morosely at Mama's lonely, proud figure in the dock.

She was a martyred Joan of Arc, defiant still, but strangely humbled by the long spell in hospital, the inexorable processes of the law which had followed and the days spent within a barred cell.

She looked like a wild bird who had been caught and caged. She had just started to accept captivity, but she would never sing or do tricks for her new masters.

Ethel, Grass, Trucker, Soapy, Dirty Dick and Little Ed felt the stinging sense of guilt as the prosecuting counsel made his last appeal to the jury. They had abandoned her in panic and fear, leaving her for dead and scurrying away like rats for the safety of their holes.

...But Mama had not been dead. Her legs crushed, she had laid in the blood of Danny and the lorry driver until the police arrived. The driver survived for five days in hospital...long enough to give the police the whole story.

The prosecutor's voice droned on and on, occasionally rising in pitch to emphasise the brutal and anti-social nature of the crime. The jury could not help but be moved in anger and indignation. There was virtually no defence. It was a predestined verdict.

The jury took only two minutes to reach their decision. They filed slowly back into the jury box, grim-faced but glowing with the inner pride of justice done.

The judge stood, resplendent in his wig and robes, and the full majesty of the law.

'Elaine Mary Willsman,' he intoned slowly. 'You have been found guilty of armed robbery...a serious crime in itself. Under other circumstances I might be inclined to leniency as this was your first offence, but society can not ignore the fact that your actions caused the violent deaths of two persons. Your chosen way of life seems to have been dangerous and detrimental to the orderly running of society. This country will not, and cannot tolerate the existence of armed gangs, young thugs whose sole pleasure in life is the destruction of things we hold dear. With all these considerations in mind, I feel that I must make an example of you in order to protect society. I hereby imprison you to the maximum penalty of twelve years imprisonment.'

An excited buzz of conversation broke out in the public galleries.

The Angels stared at Elaine's lonely figure blankly, stunned with shock. Twelve years! It was a lifetime.

As the sentence was passed, Mama's proud, defiant figure seemed to slump suddenly with resignation and horror. Her knuckles blanched as she gripped the edge of the dock as though to support herself.

She turned, staring up into the gallery with a white, frightened, accusing face.

'You bastards,' she screamed shrilly. 'You lousy bastards broke the code...you ran, you yellow pigs.'

Two constables stepped forward quickly to grasp her. Still screaming, they pinioned her arms behind her back and led her away.

With a last, defiant gesture, Mama twisted free from the imprisoning arms and turned once more to face her compatriots.

'Juice...make 'em pay,' she screamed. 'Make the bastards pay for me.'

Her screams gradually faded away down the long corridor.

It was over.

Also available from Redemption Books

Countess Dracula

by Michel Parry

"Reluctantly, they parted their bodies. Her hand found his and held it tightly as he hesitated in the doorway. He blew her one last kiss and was gone.

The ***Countess*** moved slowly to the small window and peered up at the vivid moon. Her cheeks were flushed red with excitement and apprehension. She bit her lip to stop it quivering.

Tomorrow, she foresaw, she would feast on his young body. And she would make love as she had not done in twenty years."

Filmed by Hammer this story is loosely based on the infamous Countess Elizabeth Bathory, the real life vampire who bathed in the blood of virgins in order to preserve her youth.

Price £7.99 RBKS 001

SPECIAL ILLUSTRATED EDITION

Also available from Redemption Books

Little Orphan Vampires

by Jean Rollin

"Now they wanted to find a throat to cut, a tender stomach to slit open with their sharp teeth, a plump pair of buttocks for them to sink their fangs into, like hungary young wolves. Just thinking about it made them lick their purple lips with their pink tongues. It was as though they already felt the hot, sticky liquid flowing down inside them...
Their eyes, filled before with the simple joys of seeing, now became cruel and alert like those of night-hunting beasts. The *little orphan vampires* dragged themselves up onto the cemetery wall and looked down over Paris..."

Film director Jean Rollin's latest vampire saga — due for release in 1996, is based on this book which he also wrote. First English edition.

Price £7.99   RBKS 004

SPECIAL ILLUSTRATED EDITION

COUNTESS DRACULA
QUEEN OF BLOOD

LIMITED EDITION OF 2,000 CARD SET — 10 COLOUR GORE SOAKED IMAGES.

Each set contains 10 *full colour* photographs (157mm x 200mm) of blood drenched wenches and the wicked Countess. These original and exclusive cards are based on interpretations of scenes contained in the book *Countess Dracula* by Michel Parry, published by Redemption Books.

Concept / Art Direction — Nigel Wingrove
Photography — Chris Bell
Stylist — Spencer Horne
Hair and Make up — Ashley Mae
Models:
Countess Dracula — Eileen Daly
Gypsy Woman — Maria
Peasant Woman — Marie Harper

© REDEMPTION FILMS 1995

To order send a cheque for £9.99, plus £1.00 p & p, payable to Redemption Books, to THE REDEMPTION CENTRE, PO BOX 50, STROUD, GLOUCS., ENGLAND, GL6 8YG.